LET'S DO IT AGAIN!

by Chaim Finkelstein

CIS
P·U·B·L·I·S·H·E·R·S
New York · London · Jerusalem

Copyright 1993

Published and Distributed
in the U.S., Canada and overseas by:
C.I.S. Publishers and Distributors
180 Park Avenue, Lakewood, NJ 08701
(732) 905-3000 Fax: (732) 367-6666

Book and Cover Design: Deenee Cohen
Cover Illustration: Richard Martin
Typography: Nechamie Miller

ISBN 1-56062-209-1 hard cover

PRINTED IN THE UNITED STATES OF AMERICA

Table of Contents

1   A Piece of Cake 9

2   The Perfect Gift 27

3   Watch This Pitch 41

4   A Speck of Dust 57

5   Little Sisters 81

6   Missing Pieces 99

7   Super Great 114

8   Butterflies 142

9   The Old Clunker 162

10 Mazel Tov 180

11 Let's Learn 196

CHAPTER

ONE

A Piece of Cake

"Strike one!" came the shout from the front lawn of 121 Sleepy Hollow Lane.

Gavriel Weintraub stood crouched low on the grass, with his baseball glove in hand, awaiting the next pitch from his brother Binyamin.

The sun was beginning to set, and even the busiest of streets in the town of Riverport began to grow quiet as people headed indoors on this Sunday evening.

"Come on, Gavriel," Binyamin cried. "Wake up! You're hardly paying attention. You almost let that last pitch go right by you."

"Okay, okay," Gavriel answered. "I'm paying attention. Just throw the ball."

It wasn't that Gavriel didn't like baseball. Just the past summer, he had won a trophy for hitting a record six home runs in camp. Today, however, he had something else on his mind. He was thinking about his band.

Only a few days earlier, the Cheery Bim Band had played together on stage for their very first time. Their performance at the *Lag Baomer* street fair had been a great success, and now, Gavriel's mind was full of great plans for what he hoped would be their second performance.

"*Strike two!*"

Gavriel didn't move.

"Come on, Gavriel," Binyamin cried anxiously. "Baseball season will be here soon, and I really need the practice."

Binyamin didn't just like baseball, he loved baseball. He kept his bat and glove polished all year round. Not a day went by that he didn't think of his favorite game, not even on the coldest winter day was this game forgotten. Once the slightest hint of spring poked through the cold, he would begin to beg his older brother Gavriel to come outside and help him practice his pitching.

"All right, Binyamin," Gavriel called. "Burn another one in."

"Okay," Binyamin cried as he slowly raised the ball. "Here goes."

The ball flew straight as an arrow from Binyamin's hand into the center of Gavriel's glove.

"Wow, that was a great pitch," Gavriel said as he tossed back the ball.

"Gavriel . . . Binyamin . . ." came the cry from the kitchen window. "Supper's ready."

Let's Do It Again!

"Oh no," Binyamin cried, "just when I was really starting to throw well."

"Don't worry," Gavriel said. "Soon it will be summer, and you'll have plenty of time to throw that ball around."

"I know," Binyamin answered, "but I just can't wait. One more throw before we go inside, okay?"

"All right, but make it fast. I'm hungry, and I don't want to eat a cold supper."

It wasn't long before the boys were sitting around the kitchen table with the rest of the Weintraub family.

"Gavriel and Binyamin were playing baseball today," said Miriam, the boys' nineteen-year-old sister. "I guess that's a sure sign that summer is right around the corner."

"I don't know if it's such a sure sign," chuckled Mr. Weintraub. "It seems I've seen Binyamin fooling around with that glove every day of the year."

"Well, I like baseball," Binyamin cried. "It's a great game. What could be wrong with it?"

"It's true, it's a great game," agreed his father, "and as long as you don't neglect important things like your learning, there's nothing wrong with it. That reminds me, how's your nightly learning *seder* with Shaya coming, Gavriel?"

"It's coming along just great," Gavriel answered. "We're almost finished with the first *perek* already."

"That's terrific," said Mr. Weintraub with a smile. "I'm really proud of you. Before you know it, it will be time for your *bar-mitzvah*. And won't we be proud when you make a *siyum* on the entire *Mesechte Megillah*."

Gavriel blushed.

"By the way, boys," Mr. Weintraub continued, "you both made me very proud today for another reason. The whole day people kept coming over to me to tell me how great they thought your band's performance was at the street fair."

"That's great!" Gavriel cried, perking up at the mention of the band.

"How come you're home so early tonight?" Dassie asked. "You usually eat supper at the nursing home."

"Well," answered Mr. Weintraub as he ruffled the six-year-old's hair, "many residents at the home had relatives to keep them company tonight, so I thought it would be nice to come home early and spend some time with my wonderful family."

"Oh," Mrs. Weintraub suddenly cried, "I forgot to tell everyone the good news."

"What good news?" Binyamin asked.

"Well," she continued, "do you remember what Mr. Kramer told us about the *Hachnassas Sefer Torah* that his *shul* will be celebrating?"

Gavriel's ears perked up once again.

"Yes," answered Mr. Weintraub.

"Well," Mrs. Weintraub continued with a smile, "Mr. Kramer called me this afternoon to tell me that the *simchah* will be celebrated a week from this coming Thursday, three days before *Shavuos*."

"That's great!" Binyamin shouted.

"I can't wait," Miriam agreed.

"I hope they have good cake and nosh!" little Dassie exclaimed.

"Speaking of cake, would you like some dessert, Gavriel?" asked Mrs. Weintraub, holding out a slice of chocolate cake.

There was no answer.

"Gavriel?" she asked again.

"Oh, I'm sorry, Mommy. I guess I wasn't paying attention. What did you say?"

"I just asked if you wanted a piece of cake," his mother answered. "Is something on your mind, Gavriel?"

"I'm not sure yet," Gavriel answered. "I have this idea brewing in the back of my head."

"Another idea?" Binyamin chuckled. "Here we go again!"

"Try to think about this idea later," Mrs. Weintraub said. "Right now, just try to concentrate on finishing your supper, okay?"

"Okay," Gavriel answered as he dabbed his finger into the chocolate icing on his piece of cake.

Gavriel glanced up at the clock on the kitchen wall. It was ten to eight, and he would soon have to leave to Shaya's house for their nightly study session.

I might as well leave now, he told himself. It certainly couldn't hurt if I came early. Gavriel grabbed his coat and headed for the door.

"Hmm," he said as he stepped down onto the sidewalk, "this idea of mine can't wait. I'd better give Moshe Chaim Kramer a call before I go. If anyone can help me, he can."

Gavriel turned and went right back into the house.

"What's the matter, Gavriel?" his mother asked. "Did you forget something?"

"Yeah," he said. "I forgot about an important phone call I wanted to make to my friend Moshe Chaim."

He walked into the kitchen, reached for the phone and dialed. His fingers drummed impatiently against the wall as he listened to the ringing on the line.

"Come on, Moshe Chaim," he murmured, "answer the phone already. I've gotta speak to you about something really important, and I don't want to come late for my *seder* with Shaya."

"Hello?" a voice finally answered over the line.

"Hello," he responded. "This is Gavriel Weintraub. Can I please speak to Moshe Chaim?"

"Moshe Chaim," he heard Mrs. Kramer call, "you have a telephone call."

Come on, Moshe Chaim, Gavriel thought to himself. Hurry up already. It's almost five minutes to eight. I haven't come late to Shaya's house one night since we started learning together, and I don't want this to be my first time.

"Hi, Gavriel," came a familiar voice over the line. "What's up?"

"Well," Gavriel began, "I've been thinking about the band . . ."

"I've been thinking about the band, too," Moshe Chaim interrupted. "As a matter of fact, I can't stop thinking about our performance at the *Lag Baomer* street fair. We were great! We were fantastic! We were unbelievable!"

Gavriel took another nervous glance up at the clock. "Yeah, I know," he responded. "That's why I called you."

"You didn't have to call and tell me that we were great and fantastic, I already knew that." Moshe Chaim chuckled.

Gavriel frowned. "Anyway," he continued, "your grandfather called my house today to tell us about the *simchah* his *shul* will be celebrating."

"You mean the *Hachnassas Sefer Torah?*"

"Yes," Gavriel continued a little nervously, "I was thinking about it."

"What were you thinking about?" Moshe Chaim asked.

"Well," Gavriel continued, "I'm sure your grandfather wants it to be a very happy and memorable occasion, and I know how happy our music makes everybody, so I was wondering . . . maybe you could ask your grandfather as president of the *shul* . . ."

"You want me to ask him if the band can play at the *Hachnassas Sefer Torah?*" Moshe Chaim asked.

"Exactly," Gavriel answered.

"Now why didn't I think of that?" Moshe Chaim cried. "How do you always come up with these great ideas, Gavriel? Each one is better than the one before."

"So you'll ask him?" Gavriel cut in eagerly.

"I don't know," Moshe Chaim answered. "I mean I know we sound great, but do you think we're ready to play at a real *simchah?*"

"Of course we're ready," Gavriel answered. "Don't you remember how much everybody enjoyed our playing at the street fair? Your grandfather himself thought we were great."

"That's true," Moshe Chaim answered, "but maybe

my grandfather was planning on hiring a real band to play at the *shul*."

"What do you mean a real band?" Gavriel asked. "We are a real band. We played in front of hundreds of people at the street fair, didn't we? Besides, your grandfather would probably have to pay any other band a lot of money to come play."

"That's true," Moshe Chaim answered thoughtfully.

"Of course it's true," Gavriel answered. "Why should your grandfather's *shul* have to pay hundreds of dollars for musicians to come here from New York, when he can get a band from right here in Riverport for free?"

"Okay, okay," Moshe Chaim conceded. "You've convinced me, Gavriel. I'll ask my grandfather."

"Don't just ask him," Gavriel said. "Beg him. Plead with him. Do anything. Just make sure we get to play at that *simchah*."

"Do you really think he'll let us play?" Moshe Chaim asked.

"I don't know for sure," answered Gavriel. "The only thing I know is that if anyone can get our band permission to play, it's you."

"Yeah," Moshe Chaim agreed. "Why shouldn't my grandfather let us play at the *Hachnassas Sefer Torah*? We are a great band after all. It sure sounds like a lot of fun. Okay, Gavriel, you've got me all excited. I think I'll call my grandfather right now."

"That's great!" cried Gavriel.

"Should I call you right back?" Moshe Chaim asked.

Let's Do It Again!

"No," Gavriel answered. "I have to go learn with Shaya now, but I'll call you back as soon as we finish. Okay?"

"Yeah," Moshe Chaim answered. "I'll speak to you later. Good-bye."

"Mommy!" Moshe Chaim called as he hung up the phone. "Is it okay if I call Zeidie now?"

"Hmm," answered his mother. "Now that you mention it, I have a package to deliver to your grandfather. Do you think you could bring it over to his house now? You could talk to him while you're there."

"Okay," said Moshe Chaim. "I'll go."

"Thank you, Moshe Chaim," said Mrs. Kramer, handing Moshe Chaim a box. "This is a blueberry pie, so please try to hold it very carefully."

"Don't worry. I will."

"Good," said Mrs. Kramer. "And also keep in mind that it's getting late. Please try not to take too long, okay?"

"I don't want to take too long," answered Moshe Chaim. "I've got lots of things to do when I get back."

Moshe Chaim slipped on his jacket, grabbed the package from his mother and dashed out the front door.

He loved to visit his grandfather, and he made the three-block trip to his house quite often.

As he jogged down the street, Moshe Chaim hardly looked where he was going. He knew these three blocks so well that he could probably walk them blindfolded.

As he ran, only one thought was on Moshe Chaim's mind — the band. He imagined himself and his friends, happily playing their instruments, as the whole town danced around the new *Sefer Torah*. This was the most important event to take place in Riverport in a long time. It really would be great if the Cheery Bim Band could be a big part of it.

Moshe Chaim looked up, and suddenly he saw a dark figure of a man standing on the sidewalk in front of him. He tried to stop himself, but he was moving too fast.

Crash!

Moshe Chaim collided with the man, and they both fell to the ground. Dazed, Moshe Chaim stood up, dusted himself off and looked around to see whom he had knocked down. Moshe Chaim was horrified to see a man lying on the sidewalk. He couldn't see his face at all, because it was covered with blueberry pie. In fact, much of the man's body was covered with blueberries.

"I'm sorry, sir," Moshe Chaim said nervously as he helped the man up. "Are you okay?"

The mysterious person struggled to his feet and wiped his face.

"Yes, yes," the man said. "I'm quite fine, thank you."

Moshe Chaim looked at the small, bent-over figure. This was a very old man indeed.

A large black *yarmulka* sat atop his shiny, bald head. On the tip of his nose rested a pair of small black spectacles. The lips below his white mustache were bent into an angry frown. He was obviously quite upset to have been knocked down and covered with blueberries.

Let's Do It Again!

The old man looked at Moshe Chaim sternly. "You should really be more careful where you're running, young man. And why are you running so quickly in the first place?"

"I'm really sorry," said Moshe Chaim. "I was just in a hurry to get to my grandfather's house, and I didn't see you coming from behind these bushes."

"You should be sorry," said the man angrily. "From now on, pay more attention to where you're going."

"Yes, sir," Moshe Chaim replied meekly.

The man stomped up the front stairs to his house and slammed the door shut, leaving a trail of blueberries behind him.

Boy, thought Moshe Chaim to himself. I don't know why he was so angry. It was an accident, after all, and I did say that I was sorry.

Moshe Chaim picked up as much of the pie as he could and dumped it into the nearest garbage can. Then he continued on his way to his grandfather's house at a much slower pace than before. In a few minutes, his sticky, blueberry-stained finger was ringing his grandfather's doorbell.

"Hello, Moshe Chaim," said Mr. Kramer as he opened the door. "A pleasure as always to see my grandson, but what brings you to my house at such a late hour?"

"First of all," said Moshe Chaim, "I came to deliver a blueberry pie for my mother."

"Oh, thank you very much, Moshe Chaim. I've been looking forward to that pie all day. Where is it?"

"I'm sorry, Zeidie," Moshe Chaim moaned sadly. "I

dropped it on the way here."

"Don't worry, Moshe Chaim," said Mr. Kramer. "How about if I won't breathe a word of it to your mother. I'll tell her it was one of her best blueberry pies, as far as empty calories go."

He winked at Moshe Chaim who couldn't help but smile back. Leave it to Zeidie to make him laugh over a broken pie.

"Now, young man, I can see there's something else you want to ask me."

"Well," said Moshe Chaim, "I was just speaking to my friend Gavriel Weintraub, and we were talking about the *Hachnassas Sefer Torah* that your *shul* will be having."

"Ah, yes," Mr. Kramer smiled. "Everyone in my *shul* can't wait until we get our new *Sefer Torah*. There will be such happiness when it arrives. The whole neighborhood is coming. We'll sing and dance all day around our precious, new *Sefer Torah*."

Moshe Chaim smiled. "That's exactly what I wanted to talk to you about, Zeidie."

"What do you mean?" asked Mr. Kramer.

"Well," Moshe Chaim began, "you said you want to sing and dance around the *Sefer Torah*, and to sing and dance really well you usually need music."

"Go on," said Mr. Kramer.

"Well," said Moshe Chaim, "I just happen to know of a band that could play great music for free."

"And what is the name of this band?" asked Mr. Kramer, a smile beginning to play around the corners of his mouth.

Let's Do It Again!

"Oh, Zeidie," Moshe Chaim cried. "You know which band I'm talking about, the band that I'm part of, the Cheery Bim Band."

"Oh," chuckled Mr. Kramer. "You mean that band? Why didn't you say so?"

"So, Zeidie?" Moshe Chaim asked eagerly. "Can our band play?"

"That is a very good question, Moshe Chaim," said his grandfather. "I do think that it's a very good idea, but the answer is that I just don't know."

"What do you mean?" Moshe Chaim cried. "Don't you think we're a good band? Didn't you hear how nicely we played at the street fair? Everyone loved the way we played."

"Yes, Moshe Chaim," agreed his grandfather. "You boys really did play beautifully. I was very proud of you."

"Then why don't you know if we can play at the *Hachnassas Sefer Torah*?"

"Because," answered Mr. Kramer, "it's not up to me whether you can play or not. The person who makes decisions for such events is Mr. Fineman."

"Who's he?" asked Moshe Chaim.

"Mr. Fineman is the president of our *shul* committee, and if you want your band to play in our *shul*, you're going to have to speak to him."

"Okay," said Moshe Chaim. "If you'll give me his address, I'll go speak to him tomorrow."

Mr. Kramer took out a pen from his pocket and scribbled the address on a piece of paper.

"Here it is, Moshe Chaim. It's getting late, and you'd

21

better start heading home."

"Okay, Zeidie. Thanks a lot. Good-bye."

"Good-bye, Moshe Chaim."

Meanwhile, the learning at Shaya's house was not going too smoothly.

"So, Gavriel," said Shaya, "can you think of an answer to my question?"

"What?" Gavriel asked. "Oh, I'm sorry, Shaya. I didn't hear what you said. I was just thinking about the phone call I made before I came here tonight."

"What phone call?" Shaya asked.

"I called Moshe Chaim and asked him to phone his grandfather to see if our band could play at his *shul's* *Hachnassas Sefer Torah* next Thursday."

"Aha!" Shaya shouted. "I knew you came up with another great idea tonight. I could tell by your face when you walked in.

"You know," he continued, "I think the *Hachnassas Sefer Torah* is the perfect place for us to play."

The boys' conversation was suddenly interrupted when Shaya's father, Rabbi Ginsberg, entered the room.

"How's the learning coming, boys?" he asked.

"Well," Gavriel answered, trying to remember what they had been learning, "Shaya just asked a very good question."

With that, the boys began a heated conversation with Rabbi Ginsberg about the *Gemara* they were learning.

He liked Shaya's question and showed the boys

how and where they could find the answer.

Rabbi Ginsberg was very proud of his son's nightly learning session with Gavriel, and he was always glad to be of help to the boys in any way he could.

When he left the room, the boys continued learning for a few minutes longer.

Suddenly, to Gavriel's great surprise, Shaya stopped and closed his *Gemara*.

"What are you doing?" Gavriel asked.

"What do you mean what am I doing?" Shaya answered. "We finished the piece of *Gemara*, and our hour is up."

"What?" Gavriel cried. "I've been here for an hour? It feels like I just came."

"That's good," said Shaya. "They say that time flies when you're having fun, and you must have really been enjoying our learning."

"Oh," cried Gavriel. "Speaking of fun, I can't wait to find out if we'll be playing at the *Hachnassas Sefer Torah*."

"It really is a great idea," cried Shaya. "Everyone in town will be at this *simchah*, and we should have lots of fun playing. I can't wait!"

"Me neither. I have so many questions in my mind. I keep wondering about what songs we'll play and if we'll get to do any dancing."

"Wait a minute. We still don't know if Mr. Kramer will want us to play in the first place."

"Hmmm," said Gavriel thoughtfully. "That's true. Mr. Kramer might decide he wants a more experienced band, or he might decide not to have any band at all."

The Cheery Bim Band

"No band at a *Hachnassas Sefer Torah?*" Shaya asked in surprise. "How will the people dance around the new *Sefer Torah*, if there's no music playing?"

"We dance pretty well on *Simchas Torah* without any music," Gavriel noted.

"Yes, but we also dance great in *yeshivah* on *Purim*, with a band playing in the background. Why don't we call Moshe Chaim and find out what happened?"

"Yeah, what are we waiting for?" Gavriel agreed. "I can't wait to hear what his grandfather said."

"Okay," said Shaya excitedly. "I'll call from the kitchen phone, and you pick up the hall phone. That way we'll both be able to speak at the same time."

Shaya went off to the kitchen to make the call.

"I can't wait for him to answer already," Gavriel whispered as the phone rang.

Click.

"Hello," Shaya said. "This is Shaya Ginsberg. Can I please speak to Moshe Chaim?"

"One moment please," Moshe Chaim's mother said.

"Moshe Chaim," Mrs. Kramer called.

There was no response.

"Moshe Chaim!" she called again, a little louder.

Still no response.

"I'm sorry," she told the boys. "He doesn't seem to hear me. I'll go see if I can find him in his room."

After what seemed like a long time, Moshe Chaim's voice finally came over the phone.

"*Nu?*" Shaya asked. "What took you so long?"

"Yeah," Gavriel added. "We've both been sitting

here on the phone for a long time."

"I'm sorry, guys," he apologized. "I was working so hard upstairs in my room that I just didn't hear my mother calling."

"What were you working on?" asked Gavriel.

"Just some stuff for the band when we play," Moshe Chaim answered evasively.

"Does that mean we're going to play at the *Hachnassas Sefer Torah*?" Gavriel and Shaya asked excitedly.

"Well," Moshe Chaim answered, "I have good news and bad news. Which news would you like to hear first?"

"Let's hear the good news first," Gavriel answered.

"Okay," said Moshe Chaim happily. "I was hoping you would pick the good news first."

He cleared his throat and began speaking in a very official sounding voice.

"Tonight," he said, "I went to my grandfather's house and asked him if we could play at the *Hachnassas Sefer Torah*." He paused just enough for effect. "My grandfather said that he thinks our band plays beautifully and that it was a wonderful idea for us to play in his *shul*."

"That's great!" Gavriel yelled with excitement.

"Yes," agreed Shaya. "But he still didn't tell us the bad news."

"Oh, yeah," said Gavriel. "I forgot about that."

"So what is the bad news?" Shaya asked.

"The bad news is that we can't play unless Mr. Fineman, the president of the *shul* committee, agrees."

"Oh!" Shaya groaned. "I knew there had to be a catch."

"So, how do we get this *shul* committee president to agree?" asked Gavriel.

"Don't worry, guys," Moshe Chaim said. "I'm going to go to Mr. Fineman's house tomorrow. Once I tell him about how great our band is, I'm sure he'll agree to let us play. This should be easy. A piece of cake."

"I hope you're right," said Shaya.

CHAPTER TWO

The Perfect Gift

It was a beautiful Monday morning. The sun was shining brightly, and the birds were singing their loudest. It was the type of morning that makes a person want to jump out of bed and greet the day with a smile. The whole town of Riverport seemed to be awake.

Lines were already forming for a cup of coffee in Gottleib's Pizza Shop. A new mop display was going up in front of Zemel's Hardware Store. Even the fish in Zimmerman's Fish Store seemed to flop around with new-found energy this morning.

Everyone in the Weintraub family had been up for a while. Everyone, that is, except for Gavriel.

"Come on, Gavriel, wake up already," Binyamin shouted at his still sleeping brother.

"Huh . . . what's going on?"

"What's going on?" Binyamin repeated in surprise. "What's going on is that we are going to be very late for school today if you don't hurry up and get out of bed."

Gavriel finally managed to pull himself out of bed, open his eyes and look at the clock.

"Oh no," he yelled. "We're really late, Binyamin. How come you didn't wake me up before?"

"What?" Binyamin asked in amazement. "You mean you didn't hear me at all? Why, I tried waking you at least ten times this morning. First, I shook you gently, then I yelled, then I screamed, but you didn't even move. I wanted to spill a cup of water on your head, but I was afraid you'd get angry."

"Well, maybe you should have," Gavriel said as he rushed to pull on his clothes. "I just couldn't fall asleep last night. I couldn't stop thinking about the *Hachnassas Sefer Torah.*"

"What were you thinking about?" asked Binyamin.

"Well," said Gavriel, "for one thing, I was thinking that maybe we should all dress the same when we play."

"You mean we should wear our band shirts?" asked Binyamin.

"Of course not," answered Gavriel. "To a big *simchah* like this we're going to have to wear our suits."

"But we don't have enough money to go buy new matching suits for the band."

"That's true," agreed Gavriel. "But I was thinking that we could all try to wear matching red ties. That should look pretty good. I really can't wait."

"Speaking of not being able to wait," said Binyamin,

motioning towards the clock, "if we wait any more, we're going to be very late for school."

"You're right!" said Gavriel. "It is very late. I guess we'd better jog to school today."

"Are you really sure that our band will be playing at the *Hachnassas Sefer Torah?*" Binyamin huffed as the two brothers jogged down the street.

"We don't know yet for sure," answered Gavriel. "We have to speak to the president of the *shul* first. Moshe Chaim is supposed to go see him today."

"Are you going with him?"

"I don't know," answered Gavriel. "Maybe I should."

Finally, after a lot of huffing and puffing, they reached Montgomery Boulevard and their *yeshivah.* They were right on time.

Gavriel was so out of breath, he could hardly *daven.* He didn't fully catch his breath until after *davening* was over.

During class, he had a very hard battle to fight. His *yetzer hara* kept telling him to think about the band. It took a lot of determination for him to fight this urge and keep his mind on what his *rebbi* was teaching.

Most of the time, Gavriel was able to succeed in the fight. He listened very carefully to what his *rebbi* had to say, and he even asked two good questions. With one glance over his left shoulder, however, Gavriel could see that his friend Moshe Chaim was not fighting such a winning battle.

Moshe Chaim hardly appeared to be listening at all. His mind was obviously someplace else. Gavriel guessed that Moshe Chaim's mind was busy thinking about their band. Luckily, Rabbi Goldsmith did not call on him to answer any questions.

The day passed by, and soon the dismissal bell was ringing.

"Are you going to go to Mr. Fineman's house now?" Gavriel asked Moshe Chaim as they left the *yeshivah* building.

"Yes," said Moshe Chaim. "I have the address in my pocket."

"Are you sure you don't need Shaya and me to come with you?"

"Of course not," answered Moshe Chaim. "This should be simple, a real piece of cake. How hard can it be to talk a nice old man into letting a great band play at a *simchah*? Everyone in town saw how well we played at the street fair last week. I'm sure he was there, too."

"Are you really sure?" asked Shaya nervously.

"Oh, all right," cried Moshe Chaim. "Come with me already. I'm sure it couldn't hurt to have you guys come along."

"So where does this Mr. Fineman live anyway?" asked Gavriel.

Moshe Chaim reached into his pocket and pulled out the scrap of paper his grandfather had given him the night before.

"He lives at 32 Greenvalley Drive."

"Say, isn't that near your grandfather's house?" asked Gavriel.

"Yes," answered Moshe Chaim. "It's only two blocks away."

The boys turned the corner of Willowbrook Drive.

Let's Do It Again!

"Hey, guys," cried Moshe Chaim. "Did you hear about the gefilte fish I caught on Friday?"

"What do you mean?" asked Gavriel. "Gefilte fish is not a kind of fish. It's a whole bunch of different things chopped up and cooked together. Where in the world would you go to catch one?"

"Why, Zimmerman's Fish Store, of course," answered Moshe Chaim.

"What are you talking about?" asked Shaya. "You can't catch a gefilte fish, even in a fish store."

"Well, I sure did," answered Moshe Chaim. "You see, this *Shabbos* we had lots of guests in our house."

"So what does that have to do with catching a gefilte fish?" asked Gavriel.

"Well," replied Moshe Chaim, "the first dish my mother serves at every *Shabbos* meal is gefilte fish, and for so many people she needed a lot of it. Therefore, she ordered a very big package of gefilte fish from Mr. Zimmerman this week. He makes it in his store, you know, and it's very delicious."

Shaya frowned. "You still didn't tell us how you caught a gefilte fish."

"Oh yeah!" cried Moshe Chaim. "Well, as I was saying, my mother ordered a very big package of gefilte fish, and a very big package of gefilte fish is very heavy."

"So?" asked Gavriel.

"So," continued Moshe Chaim, "old Mr. Zimmerman is not as strong as he used to be. After a long week of hard work in his store, he was hardly able to lift that heavy package."

"So?" asked Gavriel.

The Cheery Bim Band

"So," said Moshe Chaim, "as Mr. Zimmerman brought it out from behind the counter, he dropped it."

"And?" asked Shaya.

"And," chuckled Moshe Chaim, "when he dropped the package, I ran over and caught it before it landed on the floor. Ha ha! I caught the gefilte fish. Don't you get the joke?"

Gavriel smiled. "Oh, Moshe Chaim," he sighed.

"*Oy vey!*" groaned Shaya, slapping himself on the forehead. "Is that what you call a joke?"

"I think it's hilarious," laughed Moshe Chaim.

"Okay."

Moshe Chaim looked down the block ahead of him.

Boy, he thought to himself, when I was here last night it was almost dark, and everything seemed so spooky. Now the sun is shining, the birds are chirping, and everything looks so nice. What a difference there is between night and day.

In his mind, Moshe Chaim played back the events of the night before. He remembered how the near darkness had not bothered him at all, until that old man had suddenly appeared in his path. *Oy*, what a mess that had been.

Wait a minute! That accident had taken place on this very block. Moshe Chaim could still see patches of blueberry filling on the sidewalk. That man had gone into one of the houses on Greenvalley Drive. It couldn't have been 32 Greenvalley Drive—or could it?

Suddenly, Moshe Chaim felt a sinking feeling in his stomach. The patches of pie filling were on the sidewalk right next to that address. Could the old man have been Mr. Fineman? Come to think of it, his face had looked a little familiar. Could Moshe Chaim have seen him in his grandfather's *shul*?

Moshe Chaim felt his stomach churning faster than a washing machine. If the old man he had knocked over had indeed been Mr. Fineman, then the Cheery Bim Band was in deep trouble. That man had been very angry. Moshe Chaim could just imagine himself and his friends being thrown out of the man's house.

"*Oy vey*," he groaned. "Of all the people in the world, why did I have to smash a blueberry pie into the face of the one person who can let the band play?"

"What's the matter, Moshe Chaim?" Gavriel asked. "You don't look so good."

"Look!" cried Shaya. "There's an old lady watering plants on the porch of the house. It must be Mrs. Fineman."

Plants? Suddenly, Moshe Chaim had an idea.

"Follow me, guys," he cried as he began running down the street.

"What's going on?" Gavriel and Shaya asked as they ran after him. "Didn't we just pass Mr. Fineman's house?"

"Yes, we did," Moshe Chaim answered. "But we have to go somewhere else first."

"Where in the world are we going?" asked the boys as they chased after him.

"To pick some flowers," he answered.

"What?"

"Don't worry," said Moshe Chaim. "We only have

one more block to go until we reach my grandfather's house. I'll explain everything when we get there."

It didn't take long for the boys to reach Mr. Kramer's house.

"Where's Moshe Chaim?" Shaya asked Gavriel.

"I don't know," answered Gavriel. "He was right in front of us a minute ago."

Suddenly, Moshe Chaim emerged from his grandfather's house with garden shears in his hands.

"Don't worry, guys," he said. "My grandfather said it's okay to cut some of the flowers from his front lawn."

"Why would we want to do that?" asked Shaya.

"Yeah," cried Gavriel. "Come on, Moshe Chaim, tell us what's going on."

"Okay," said Moshe Chaim sheepishly as he headed towards a tall bush with fragrant purple blossoms cascading down its sides. "Let me tell you what happened to me last night."

As Moshe Chaim cut down some of the sweet-smelling flower clusters, he told his friends about the accident of the night before.

"Oh," said Shaya. "I guess that explains why I saw dark blue stains all over the sidewalk back there."

"Yes," said Gavriel. "But it doesn't explain why we need flowers."

"Well," said Moshe Chaim, "if the man I knocked down last night really was Mr. Fineman, then he's going to be very angry with me. I figured that maybe if we brought a little present, Mr. Fineman wouldn't be so upset."

"Oh," said Gavriel. "I get it. When you saw Mrs.

Fineman watering the flowers, you figured she would like flowers, too."

"Exactly," answered Moshe Chaim as they walked back towards the Fineman house. "My mother always says that flowers are the perfect gift. Do you think these look nice?"

"I guess so," said Gavriel. "What do you think, Shaya?"

"I don't know anything about flowers. What I do know is that we're wasting a lot of time. We're not even sure if the man Moshe Chaim hit was Mr. Fineman, and even if it was, we don't know if he will still be angry. Let's just go inside already."

Gavriel and Moshe Chaim nodded, and the three boys slowly walked up the stairs to the house.

Moshe Chaim nervously reached out his finger and rang the doorbell.

As the door opened, the boys were all quite relieved to see a tall, young man with dark brown hair standing before them.

"Hi," began Moshe Chaim. "Are you Mr. Fineman?"

"Yes," answered the man. "Can I help you?"

The boys all let out a sigh of relief. This was most certainly not the same person that Moshe Chaim had knocked over the night before.

"Well," said Moshe Chaim, "we're the members of the Cheery Bim Band, and we came to speak to you about us playing at your *shul's Hachnassas Sefer Torah* next week."

"Yes," added Gavriel. "We were told that you are the president of the *shul* committee and that you're the one we should ask about letting us play."

"Oh," exclaimed the man, motioning them inside as he walked towards the next room. "You must want to speak to my father. I'll go get him."

"His father?" Moshe Chaim whispered. "Uh oh!"

Thirty seconds later, a short, bald, familiar-looking figure hobbled into the room. Moshe Chaim let out a groan as he recognized the man from the night before.

Mr. Fineman hobbled over to a large stuffed chair and sat down. He gestured towards the couch.

"Have a seat, boys," he said.

The boys nervously found seats.

Mr. Fineman peered over the top of his glasses. Slowly, he studied the faces of each boy before him.

Suddenly, his eyes fell upon Moshe Chaim.

"You!" he cried. "You're that wild boy who crashed into me last night. Because of you, my back hurts, and my favorite brown pants are covered with blueberry stains. Have you come to do some more damage?"

Moshe Chaim felt his heart turn to jelly. "No," he stammered. "I wanted to say I was sorry for what happened last night."

"Hmmph, are you sure you didn't come back to give me a karate chop or something?"

Suddenly, the boys heard a voice from behind them.

"Shlomo Fineman!" cried Mrs. Fineman. "Why are you being so strict with such a nice, young man? If he bumped into you last night, it was probably an accident. He said he was sorry. He doesn't mean you any harm."

Let's Do It Again!

"That's right!" cried Moshe Chaim, jumping up and holding out his flowers to Mrs. Fineman. "I even brought you a present."

"Oh, how sweet," said Mrs. Fineman. "Let me see. What kind of flowers are these, anyway?"

Moshe Chaim stretched out his arm, bringing the bouquet directly in front of Mrs. Fineman's face.

Suddenly, she let out a scream.

"Oh no!" she cried, "these flowers are . . . hatchoo . . . lilacs . . . hatchoo . . . How terrible! I'm so very . . . hatchoo . . . allergic to lilacs!"

With that, Mrs. Fineman ran out of the room, sneezing all the way.

Mr. Fineman glared at Moshe Chaim.

"I'll be right back," he said threateningly as he hobbled after his wife.

Moshe Chaim sunk his head down into his lap. "I guess flowers aren't always the perfect gift after all."

"We're doomed!" groaned Shaya.

"We're double doomed!" cried Moshe Chaim.

"Well," sighed Gavriel, "so much for the Cheery Bim Band playing at the *Hachnassas Sefer Torah*."

"What do you think Mr. Fineman will do to us?" whispered Shaya.

"I don't know," answered Moshe Chaim. "First, I clobbered him with a pie, and then I put his wife into a sneezing fit. If I were him, I would probably pick all of us up and throw us out the window."

"Maybe he'll call the police," said Shaya nervously.

"Calm down, guys," said Gavriel. "Are you forgetting that Mr. Fineman is the president of the Beis Knesses

Hagadol *shul* committee? Anyone who is such an important member of a *shul* couldn't get that angry at us."

"Oh no?" said Moshe Chaim. "Did you see the way he looked at me when his wife started sneezing? I thought he was going to hit me with his cane."

"Maybe we should just sneak out of the house now before he comes back."

"Too late," whispered Gavriel. "I can hear Mr. Fineman coming now."

The boys sat quietly, their hearts beating more loudly than ever before. Slowly, Mr. Fineman shuffled back over to his seat. He sat down and glared silently at the boys in front of him. The boys felt their hearts beating faster by the second.

What can he be thinking? Gavriel thought nervously. I know. I bet he already called the police and is waiting for them to come.

Shaya had taken off his glasses and was rubbing his eyes frantically.

Moshe Chaim wasn't moving a muscle. He sat very still, keeping a close eye on Mr. Fineman's cane. I'd better get ready to run, he thought to himself.

The room was very quiet, way too quiet for the three nervous boys sitting on the couch. They listened to the ticking of the clock as Mr. Fineman continued to glare at them.

Finally, Moshe Chaim decided to break the silence. He swallowed hard, took a deep breath and began to speak.

"I'm really sorry, Mr. Fineman," he stammered. "I

had no idea that your wife was allergic to lilacs. I didn't mean to make her sick."

Gavriel and Shaya breathed a sigh of relief, now that the horrible silence had been broken.

Mr. Fineman put down his cane and began to speak.

"Who are you, boys?" he asked. "And just why have you come to visit me?"

"Well," began Moshe Chaim, "I'm Moshe Chaim Kramer, and these are my friends Gavriel Weintraub and Shaya Ginsberg. We heard about the *Hachnassas Sefer Torah* your *shul* will be having, and we wanted to know if our band could play the music for it. My grandfather, Mr. Kramer, said that we would have to ask you."

"Oh," said Mr. Fineman, finally breaking his silence. "Your grandfather is Mr. Kramer. He is a very fine man. I don't know where he got such a grandson though. Has this band of yours ever played anywhere before?"

"Yes, we have, sir," answered Gavriel. "Just last week we played at the *Lag Baomer* street fair. I'm sure you must have heard about our performance. Everyone in town is still talking about it."

"No," Mr. Fineman snapped. "I haven't heard about your performance, but I will most certainly research the matter and find out how well you played. I will also speak to Mr. Kramer himself and see what his feelings are on the matter. Come back tomorrow at this time, and I'll give you my answer. Good day, young men." Mr. Fineman motioned towards the door with his cane.

"Thank you, Mr. Fineman," Moshe Chaim said uncertainly as he headed for the door with his friends. "Thank you very much."

"There's no need to thank me," said Mr. Fineman. "I don't believe in extending favors to boys like you. I'm only giving you a small chance, because if I don't, your grandfather will be after me to find out why I didn't."

The three boys quickly ran down the front stairs of the house and began to run up the block. They didn't stop until they were far away from 32 Greenvalley Drive. When they were sure they were out of earshot, they stopped to look at each other uncertainly.

"Do you think we have a chance?" Moshe Chaim asked mournfully.

"Who knows?" Gavriel answered. "I guess we'll find out tomorrow."

CHAPTER THREE

Watch This Pitch

"Gavriel," began Binyamin, on the way to school Tuesday morning, "are you sure Yossi and I have to come with you to Mr. Fineman's house?"

Yossi was Binyamin's best friend as well as the fifth member of the Cheery Bim Band.

"Yes," answered Gavriel. "Mr. Fineman is in charge of the committee that will decide whether our band will play at his *shul* function. If they decide to let us play, he will most certainly want to meet the rest of the band."

"So," complained Binyamin, "why can't we wait until he decides for sure? Yossi and I were planning on practicing our pitching and catching tonight."

"We probably could," said Gavriel. "But Shaya and I discussed this, and we really think Mr. Fineman might become more impressed with our band if he sees all five of us. Practice your pitching some other time."

"But we're having our first big game on Sunday after school."

"Don't worry so much," said Gavriel. "I'm sure you'll find some time to practice."

Suddenly, Binyamin had an idea. "Yeah," he said. "I know just when we'll be able to."

That day, the sixth grade of Toras Moshe Yeshivah spent every free moment discussing the upcoming baseball game. It was to be the first of the season, and everyone was excited. In the yard, during recess, the two teams were chosen. Binyamin and Yossi were overjoyed to learn that they would be on the same team. Binyamin would pitch, while Yossi would catch.

"Where are we going to practice tonight?" Yossi asked Binyamin as they walked back to their class-room after recess. "On your front lawn or mine?"

"Neither one," answered Binyamin.

"Then where do you want to practice? In Castle Park?"

"Nope," answered Binyamin.

"Just tell me already," Yossi cried. "Where are we going to be practicing tonight?"

"Well," said Binyamin, "Gavriel says that we have to go along with the rest of the band when they go speak to Mr. Fineman, the president of Beis Knesses Hagadol *shul* committee. He thinks that if all the members of the band come along, it will help our chances of getting the job, if anything can. I guess Mr. Fineman wasn't very impressed with Moshe Chaim last night. Gavriel thinks that if we all go today, maybe it will help."

Let's Do It Again!

"I guess it's worth a try," agreed Yossi. "After what happened in Mr. Fineman's house last night, we're going to need all the help we can get for him to let us play. I guess we won't be able to practice at all tonight."

"I'm not so sure about that," said Binyamin. "Whoops, Rebbi just walked in. We'll have to wait until later to talk."

When school was over, all five members of the Cheery Bim Band met in front of the *yeshivah* building.

"Now remember, everybody," Gavriel announced. "Let's try to be very nice when we meet with Mr. Fineman. He is the one in charge of letting our band play at the big *simchah*."

"Yeah," added Moshe Chaim. "And let's try to be careful, too. If we make any more trouble for this man, he'll probably call the police or something."

"What trouble could we possibly get into?" asked Binyamin. "We're not bringing any pies or flowers this time."

"Let's just try to be careful anyway," said Shaya. "My mother always tells me that a person can never be too careful."

"Say," began Moshe Chaim, "do you think you guys could come to my house after we finish with Mr. Fineman?"

"Why?" asked Shaya.

"I wanted to show you the great stuff I made for the band."

"What kind of great stuff?" asked Gavriel.

"I don't want to tell you now," answered Moshe

Chaim. "I want you to be surprised when you see it."

"I hope you didn't put too much work into this stuff," said Shaya. "After all, we still don't know if Mr. Fineman is going to let us play, remember?"

"I know," said Moshe Chaim. "But this is stuff the band can use any time we play."

"Okay," said Gavriel. "I guess we can come see your surprise, Moshe Chaim. I don't think any of us has to be home before seven o'clock anyway. Right, guys?"

The other boys nodded their heads.

"Speaking of surprises," said Shaya, "what's in that bag you're holding, Binyamin?"

"This?" said Binyamin, holding up a white shopping bag. "This is my baseball and glove."

"Why did you take them with you?" asked Gavriel.

"So I could practice my pitching, of course."

"What? Where on earth are you planning to do that?"

"Right here, and right now," answered Binyamin.

"Catch, Yossi!" he yelled as he tossed his friend the glove. "You run ahead down the block, and I'll pitch the ball to you as we walk."

"That's a great idea!" cried Yossi. "Now we can practice our baseball and visit Mr. Fineman at the same time."

"Binyamin," said Gavriel nervously, "I don't think that this is such a good idea."

"What's wrong with it?" asked Binyamin as he let loose a zooming fastball.

"You're not supposed to play baseball in the street. You could hit someone or something really hard with that fastball of yours."

"Don't worry, Gavriel," cried Binyamin. "I'm a great pitcher. I can hit the exact center of the strike zone every time. I won't let this ball hit anything or anyone else except the inside of the glove on Yossi's hand. Watch!"

Binyamin threw a rocket-fast pitch to the glove on Yossi's hand.

"Wow!" cried Yossi as the ball smacked into the glove. "That was your best pitch yet, Binyamin. I hope you do as well at our game next week."

"That was nothing," said Binyamin confidently. "Watch this pitch. I'm going to throw it with one eye shut."

Binyamin closed one eye and let loose with a pitch so fast that it looked like a blur as it zoomed by.

"Wow!" cried Yossi. "That was an amazing pitch."

"Yes, it was," agreed Gavriel. "But you'd better put that ball away now, Binyamin. That's Mr. Fineman's house over there."

"Okay," said Binyamin. "Let me just show you guys one more pitch. I'm going to throw another perfect strike, but this time both my eyes will be closed."

Gavriel tried to stop his brother. "No!" he cried. "Don't do it, Binyamin!"

But it was too late. The ball was already on its way out of Binyamin's hands. This time, however, it was not headed straight for Yossi's glove.

To the horror of all the boys, the ball appeared to be on a direct course for the window in the door of Mr. Fineman's house.

Suddenly, the door opened, and there stood Mr. Fineman directly in the path of the oncoming ball.

"Oh, no!" cried Moshe Chaim. "Not again!"

He was sure the ball would hit Mr. Fineman right on the head. If that happened, the band would certainly not be allowed to play at the *Hachnassas Sefer Torah*. In fact, he would most certainly expect Mr. Fineman to call the police.

The boys were about to close their eyes when Mr. Fineman suddenly lifted up a large watering can and began to water the plants hanging above his front porch. The boys breathed a sigh of relief when the ball hit the watering can instead of Mr. Fineman's head. The whole incident had taken no more than a second.

Their relief was short-lived, though, since unfortunately, the force of Binyamin's pitch made the can fly through the air, spilling most of its contents on Mr. Fineman.

Mr. Fineman wiped his dripping face and turned slowly towards the boys.

"That's it," whispered Moshe Chaim. "We're doomed."

"Mr. Kramer," cried the old man between gritted teeth as he glared at Moshe Chaim, "do you enjoy attacking my wife and me? First, you knocked me down and hit me with a pie, then you sent my wife into a sneezing fit, and now you gave me a shower. What are you going to try to do next?"

Moshe Chaim didn't know what to say.

"I'm really sorry, sir," he stammered.

"It was my fault, sir," said Binyamin stepping

forward. "The other boys warned me not to throw the ball, and I threw it anyway. I'm really sorry."

"And just who are you?" Mr. Fineman asked coldly.

"I'm Binyamin Weintraub, Gavriel's brother, and this is my friend Yossi Belsky. We're also members of the Cheery Bim Band. I didn't mean to hit you with my ball."

"Well," sputtered Mr. Fineman, "I can see that you fit in quite nicely with this group of young ruffians."

Mr. Fineman motioned the boys closer as he wiped his face with his handkerchief.

"So," he asked coldly, "is this the whole Cheery Bim Band?"

"Yes, sir," answered Gavriel.

The boys fidgeted nervously, as Mr. Fineman paused to examine them closely.

"This morning," he said, "I spoke to Mr. Kramer, and he highly recommends his grandson's band, as was to be expected."

Moshe Chaim smiled nervously.

"I also inquired with some friends of mine, and they said that you boys played very nicely at the *Lag Baomer* street fair."

"Does that mean we have the job?" asked Gavriel.

"Well," said Mr. Fineman, "I wouldn't go that far. There are still the remaining members of the *shul* committee to speak with. I have arranged a meeting to discuss the matter. We will be meeting at the *shul* in half an hour. I would suggest that you call Mr. Kramer in about an hour. As the *shul* president, he will be attending this meeting, and he should know the decision by that time. I just want you boys to be aware, though, where you stand with me. The opinion that I will state is that a band of young ruffians like you should not be allowed to play at such an auspicious occasion as our *shul's Hachnassas Sefer Torah.* Of course, even though I am the committee president, I am only entitled to one vote, but I will of course make my opinion known. Good day, boys." Mr. Fineman nodded as he turned to go inside, firmly shutting the door behind him.

"Well," said Moshe Chaim mournfully as the boys headed down the block, "I guess I really botched this one up for us."

"Don't worry about it," Gavriel said. "Don't forget we still have your grandfather rooting for us."

"Yeah, I guess so," replied Moshe Chaim without much enthusiasm. "Anyway, we can call my grandfather soon to find out what happened. Why don't you guys come to my house now to see my surprise? We can call my grandfather from there."

"That sounds like a good idea to me," said Gavriel. "Is it okay with everyone else?"

The other boys all nodded their heads.

"Good," said Gavriel. "Let's go."

"Oh boy!" cried Moshe Chaim. "I just can't wait to show you guys the stuff I made for the band."

As they walked to Moshe Chaim's house, Gavriel's mind churned trying to figure out what Moshe Chaim's surprise could possibly be.

"What is this surprise anyway?" he asked.

"If I told you," answered Moshe Chaim, "it wouldn't

be a surprise any more."

"That's true," agreed Gavriel.

It wasn't long before the boys found themselves standing on the front steps of the Kramer house.

Gavriel stopped and looked at the large house in front of him. It was certainly a much bigger home than his. Two tall white pillars stood in front of the large wooden door. Every time Gavriel visited Moshe Chaim, he couldn't help but marvel at how beautiful his house was.

It was not that Gavriel was jealous. He was very happy with the house he lived in and wouldn't move for all the money in the world. It was just that he found this house to be a breathtaking sight.

"Let's go call my grandfather," said Moshe Chaim as they walked across the shiny marble floor.

"Why?" asked Shaya. "Mr. Fineman said that we should wait an hour first."

"Oh yeah," said Moshe Chaim.

"Why don't you show us your surprise first?" suggested Gavriel.

"Okay," said Moshe Chaim. "Come up to my room, and I'll show you."

The boys climbed the long white staircase and entered Moshe Chaim's room.

"I have two surprises to show you, guys," he said. "First," he pointed to a white sheet on the floor, "is the sign that will hang behind us when we play."

Moshe Chaim lifted the sheet to reveal a huge sign almost as big as the sheet itself.

"Wow!" gasped Gavriel.

"Amazing!" Shaya sputtered, rubbing his eyes.

"Unbelievable!" cried Yossi.

"Gorgeous!" yelled Binyamin.

Written in huge black and red letters were the words, "CHEERY BIM BAND, Music for Every Occasion."

"This way," Moshe Chaim explained, "everyone will know who we are when we play, and maybe they'll ask us to play when they have a *simchah*."

The boys didn't move. They couldn't take their eyes off the big, beautiful sign in front of them.

"My second surprise," Moshe Chaim continued, "is right here in my top drawer. I thought of this last night."

He slid the dresser drawer open and reached inside, pulling out what appeared to be a pile of small white papers.

"I got the idea for this from the band that played at my cousin's wedding two years ago."

He handed each boy a paper. On it were written the words: "Cheery Bim Band, Music for Every Occasion."

"What are these?" Gavriel asked.

"Why, they're business cards," Moshe Chaim answered.

"Business cards?" asked Shaya. "What do we need business cards for?"

"Well," Moshe Chaim answered, "we want our band to play at lots of *simchos*, right?"

"I guess so," said Shaya, nervously rubbing his eyes.

"If we want people to ask us to play at their *simchos*,

we have to let them know we play at *simchos*. We have to advertise."

"You mean you want to give these out at the *Hachnassas Sefer Torah?*"

"Exactly!" Moshe Chaim answered. "That way everyone will know to call us when they have a *simchah* of their own."

Gavriel sat down, leaned his head back and stroked an imaginary beard on his chin.

"I guess it sounds like a nice idea," he admitted. "The only question is, do we want to play at everyone's *simchah?*"

"I was just thinking the same thing," Shaya said. "Although, I have to admit, it does sound exciting."

"What's the problem?" Moshe Chaim asked.

"We have learning and homework to do every night. How will we have time to play at so many parties?"

"Oh," said Moshe Chaim quietly. "I never thought about that."

"We could experiment," Shaya suggested.

"What do you mean?" asked Gavriel.

"I mean," he answered, "we could try giving out the business cards this one time, and then we could see what happens."

"You're right, Shaya," Gavriel agreed. "What could possibly go wrong? If too many people ask us to play for them, we could just say no, right?"

"So, you guys want to give out the cards?" Moshe Chaim asked.

"I guess so," the boys answered.

"Great!" Moshe Chaim cried. "Then grab some

scissors and start cutting. I wrote two hundred of these, and we have to cut them out."

"What?" the boys cried together. "When did you write all these business cards?"

"Last night," Moshe Chaim answered.

"Well . . . we have to be home for supper in an hour."

"Don't worry," Moshe Chaim said. "If all five of us work together, it shouldn't take very long. Here." He handed each boy a pile. "I made four cards on each sheet of paper. Start cutting them out."

The boys looked at each other, shrugged their shoulders and started cutting.

"You know," Binyamin said, "this is kind of fun."

"Yeah," agreed Gavriel. "I never thought using a pair of scissors could be fun. Maybe I should become a barber."

The boys all laughed.

"I hope we get a chance to eat while we're playing at the *Hachnassas Sefer Torah*," said Moshe Chaim.

"If we get the job," answered Gavriel, "I'm sure we'll be able to sneak over to the tables of food in between songs."

"Now that you mention it," said Moshe Chaim, "what songs are we going to sing anyway?"

"Every song that we know," answered Shaya, "especially the ones we've been practicing these last few days since *Lag Baomer*."

"It's a good thing that we are able to practice our music after *Lag Baomer*," Yossi said.

"Yeah," said Binyamin. "I sure would hate to have

to play at the *Hachnassas Sefer Torah* with only one practice, like we did at the Pirchei talent contest."

"It wasn't so bad," Moshe Chaim declared. "We did a great job anyway, just like we'll do a great job this time, too."

"Sure," said Shaya. "We'll do a great job if we're given the chance, but don't forget that we need to play many more songs for a *Hachnassas Sefer Torah* than we did for the talent show. We'll certainly need all the practice we can get."

"Do you think we should make up a new song, like we did for the *Lag Baomer* street fair?" Gavriel asked.

"Of course," said Moshe Chaim. "Everybody loved the new song we sang last time."

"What's the song going to be about?" asked Binyamin.

"I think it should be a song about learning Torah," answered Gavriel. "This whole party will be in honor of the Torah after all."

One by one, the cut out cards fell to the floor.

Finally, they were all finished. On the floor sat a very tall pile of two hundred Cheery Bim Band business cards.

"They really look great," Moshe Chaim said proudly.

"Hey," Shaya shouted. "What time is it?"

"Wow," said Moshe Chaim. "It's already seven o'clock. Time really flies sometimes."

"Seven o'clock?" shouted Gavriel. "We've been here for an hour already, and I've got to go home."

"Yeah," said Shaya. "Me, too."

"Wait a minute!" cried Moshe Chaim. "I didn't call my grandfather yet."

The Cheery Bim Band

"Oh yeah," said Gavriel. "You'd better call him right now, and please try to make it fast. We're all going to be late for supper."

Moshe Chaim ran into the kitchen and dialed his grandfather's phone number. The rest of the boys waited for him in the living room.

"Do you think the *shul* committee agreed to let us play?" Binyamin asked nervously.

"I don't know," answered Gavriel. "With Mr. Fineman voting against us and Mr. Kramer for us, I don't know who's side they'll end up taking."

Suddenly, the boys were interrupted by the sound of someone clearing his throat.

"Harrumph."

They all whirled their heads around to see Moshe Chaim standing behind them.

"I just finished speaking to my grandfather," he said, a big smile on his freckled face.

"*Nu?*" said Shaya. "What did he say?"

"Well," Moshe Chaim answered, "first he told me about how proud he was of me being a part of the band."

"That's nice," pushed Shaya. "But what about the *Hachnassas Sefer Torah?*"

"As I was saying," Moshe Chaim continued, ignoring the interruption, "my grandfather told me how proud he was. He said that the last musician we had in our family was his Uncle Berel in Europe. He played the violin, you know. He also . . ."

"What about our band?" Shaya moaned impatiently.

"I'm getting to that," Moshe Chaim answered. "My grandfather told me that he had a long talk with Mr. Fineman in *shul* this morning."

"Could you please get to the point already, Moshe Chaim?" Shaya groaned through clenched teeth.

"Okay, okay. The *shul*'s committee took a vote and reached a decision."

"So, what did they decide?" Gavriel asked anxiously.

Moshe Chaim slowly smoothed his red hair and took a deep breath. "They decided," he said, "that they would love to have our music playing as they dance with their new *Sefer Torah.*"

"Yahoo!" Gavriel yelled, throwing his arms in the air.

"Yes! Yes! Yes!" Shaya shouted, as he jumped up and down.

"All right," cried Binyamin and Yossi, slapping each other on the back.

"Thanks a lot, Moshe Chaim," Gavriel said. "You came through for the band again."

"*Yasher koach!*" cried Shaya and the other boys.

Moshe Chaim blushed. "It was really nothing. Besides, don't forget that I nearly ruined the whole thing, too."

"Well the main thing is that it turned out all right," Shaya said.

"We've really got to be going now," said Gavriel, looking at his watch.

"Good night, Moshe Chaim," the boys all called as they walked out the front door. "See you tomorrow."

The Cheery Bim Band

"Good night, guys."

The door closed, and the boys headed down the street.

"Boy," said Shaya, "that poster was beautiful. Moshe Chaim must have put a lot of time and work into it."

"What about those business cards?" asked Gavriel. "He must have spent hours writing them all up."

"When did he have the time to do all that?" asked Binyamin. "How does he find time to learn and do homework?"

"That's a good question," said Gavriel thoughtfully. "A very good question."

CHAPTER FOUR

A Speck of Dust

The next morning all the members of the Cheery Bim Band walked into *yeshivah* with a song on their lips. Knowing that they were going to be playing at the *Hachnassas Sefer Torah* made them feel great.

"Good morning, Moshe Chaim," said Gavriel with a smile as the two boys walked into class together. "How do you feel today?"

"I feel great!" answered Moshe Chaim. "Ever since we learned that the band will be playing, I haven't been able to think about anything else."

"Well, at least you've finished making the posters and business cards," said Gavriel.

"Are you kidding?" laughed Moshe Chaim. "Did you actually think I was finished making those posters? I spent two hours making another one after you guys left my house last night."

The Cheery Bim Band

Gavriel looked at his friend in disbelief.

"Why on earth did you do that?" he asked.

"Because," answered Moshe Chaim, "we need lots of posters, so we can hang them up all over the *shul* while we're playing. That way everyone will know who we are."

"Don't you think one sign is enough?" asked Gavriel.

"No way," answered Moshe Chaim. "We want to make sure that every single person knows our name."

"I'm not so sure that it's such a good idea," said Gavriel. "Let's bring it up at band practice after school. We can't talk about it now anyway. Rebbi is walking into the room now."

"Okay, boys," said Rabbi Goldsmith after *davening*. "I hope you are all ready to learn, because we're going to be starting right away."

All the boys in the class began to open their *Gemaras*.

"Wait a minute, boys," said Rabbi Goldsmith. "Before we open our *Gemaras*, I think it's about time we have a review on what we've learned until now. I've even prepared a short surprise quiz with some questions about what we've been learning this year."

The boys all groaned as Rabbi Goldsmith passed out the papers.

"Don't worry. It starts with some easy questions, from the *mishnayos* we learned in the beginning of the year. The last few questions are on the new material."

Oh no, Moshe Chaim groaned to himself. I didn't know the answer to yesterday's questions on the

Let's Do It Again!

Gemara we were learning. If I get any questions wrong today he'll certainly notice, and I'll probably get into really big trouble.

He looked down at the first question: "What is the tallest height a *sukkah* is allowed to be?"

That's easy enough, he thought to himself somewhat relieved. It's in the very first *mishnah* of *Mishnayos Sukkah*.

"A *sukkah* is not allowed to be taller than twenty *amos*," he wrote.

The next few questions were just as easy. It wasn't until Moshe Chaim got towards the end of his paper, to the questions from the material they had just begun these last few weeks, that he felt his confidence start to ebb.

"According to the *mishnah*, what do we do if two witnesses testify that a *beis din* in another city ruled that a person is *chayav misah*," began the new set of questions.

Oh no, thought Moshe Chaim. I don't remember the answer to that one. What am I going to do?

He felt sure, though, that he would know the answers to most of the remaining questions. Unfortunately, he was wrong. He didn't know the answer to the next one or the one after that either.

This can't be happening, he thought to himself. I might not be the best student in the class, but I've never thought of myself as being a bad student.

Moshe Chaim didn't feel too good when he handed in his quiz. He couldn't understand why he hadn't remembered the answers to the last questions.

The Cheery Bim Band

Later that afternoon, while all the boys were at the band's first practice since they had heard the good news about the *Hachnassas Sefer Torah*, the phone rang in the Kramer house. Mr. Yehoshua Kramer, Moshe Chaim's father, answered it.

He was surprised to hear Rabbi Goldsmith's voice over the line.

"Hello, Rabbi Goldsmith," he said into the phone. "How are you?"

"*Baruch Hashem*, I am fine, thank you," Rabbi Goldsmith replied. "I called to speak to you about Moshe Chaim's learning."

"Yes, yes," replied Mr. Kramer, eagerly. "How has my Moshe Chaim's learning been coming along?"

"Well," said Rabbi Goldsmith slowly, "I'm a little worried about him. You see, Mr. Kramer, your son has *b'li ayin hara* a good head, and for most of this year his learning was excellent."

Rabbi Goldsmith paused to allow his words to sink in.

"Yes, yes," said Mr. Kramer. "Please continue."

"Well," said Rabbi Goldsmith, "as I said, Moshe Chaim's learning was excellent for most of this year. Unfortunately, he has not been learning as well as he could for the past few weeks. I can only conclude that he has stopped reviewing his learning at home."

"What?" cried Mr. Kramer. "Are you sure? I see Moshe Chaim lock himself into his room every night. I assumed he was learning in there."

"Well," replied Rabbi Goldsmith, "he is obviously not spending his time learning. Just this morning, I passed out a fairly simple quiz to the boys. He did well enough with the questions I had there from the material we learned at the beginning of the year, but once he hit the things we've been doing just these past few weeks, his memory seems to have fallen off."

"Then what has he been doing with all his free time?"

"That's a very good question," replied Rabbi Goldsmith. "I suggest you ask Moshe Chaim yourself. I am constantly hearing him talk to his friends about the band he is in. The band is only a few weeks old, and this problem of Moshe Chaim's also seems to be a relatively new one. I have a feeling that this band of his is a big part of the problem."

"Oh no," sighed Mr. Kramer. "I certainly hope not. I'll have to ask Moshe Chaim as soon as he gets home from school."

"Very good," said Rabbi Goldsmith. "I'll also try to speak with Moshe Chaim tomorrow and see what I can come up with."

"Very good. Good-bye, Rabbi Goldsmith, and thank you for your concern."

A worried furrow creased Mr. Yehoshua Kramer's brow as he hung up the phone. Moshe Chaim had always been such a good boy. His learning had never been a problem before. What was going on now? His father was very determined to find out.

That night, at the dinner table, he began to question his son.

"How was your day at school?" he asked.

"It was okay, I guess," answered Moshe Chaim.

"The boys and I are really excited about the band. We made a whole bunch of plans during recess."

"That's nice," answered Mr. Kramer. "And what did you learn today in Rabbi Goldsmith's class?"

"We didn't learn much of anything new," answered Moshe Chaim. "We spent most of the morning taking a quiz."

Mr. Kramer looked his son in the eye. "Were you able to answer the questions on the quiz?"

Sweat began to pour down Moshe Chaim's face as he thought back to the class quiz that morning. He certainly couldn't tell his father how poorly he knew he had done with those final questions.

The room suddenly seemed very quiet. The ticking of the kitchen clock was the only audible sound.

Suddenly, to Moshe Chaim's great relief, the silence was broken by a new voice. It was his mother, coming to his rescue.

"I'm sure Moshe Chaim knew his work just fine," said Mrs. Kramer, waving her spoon. "Now both of you please eat your dinner, before it gets cold."

Moshe Chaim felt like giving his mother the biggest hug. Without even knowing it, she had saved him from getting into great trouble.

Oh well, thought Mr. Kramer taking a bite of his dinner, I can see that I won't be getting any answers out of Moshe Chaim. I guess I'm going to have to do a little investigating to find out what's really going on.

When Moshe Chaim finished *bentching*, he excused himself and headed upstairs towards his room as he did every night.

Let's Do It Again!

While Mrs. Kramer cleared the table, Mr. Kramer remained in his seat pondering how to approach Moshe Chaim on the subject of his learning. What did he do up in his room each night if he wasn't learning anyway? Suddenly, a smile lit up his face. He had an idea.

He pushed his chair back and went over to the refrigerator.

"What are you doing, Yehoshua?" asked his wife as he pulled out a dish and set it down on the counter.

"I just wanted a little snack."

"A little snack?" cried Mrs. Kramer. "But we just finished eating?"

"It's not for me," answered her husband as he sliced a piece of his wife's delicious cherry cheesecake. "It's for Moshe Chaim."

"You mean to say that you think Moshe Chaim is hungry only five minutes after we've finished supper?"

"Er . . . could be," stammered Mr. Kramer as he turned to leave the room.

Mrs. Kramer was left standing in the kitchen, scratching her head in confusion as her husband headed up the stairs, carrying the piece of cheesecake.

He walked up to the door of Moshe Chaim's room and knocked.

"Come in," came Moshe Chaim's voice from inside the room.

"Here, Moshe Chaim," Mr. Kramer said as he came in. "I've brought you a little . . . snack."

Mr. Kramer stood with his mouth wide open, staring at the amazing sight before him, the plate of cheesecake in his hands forgotten.

The bed was covered with the huge black and red CHEERY BIM BAND sign. On the floor around Moshe Chaim were several poster boards he appeared to be presently working on. The floor was littered with markers and paints.

"How . . ." he began. "When did you make all these signs? Why, there must be a dozen of them, and they're all so big. I must admit, Moshe Chaim, that these signs are really beautiful, but when in the world did you have time to make them? And what about your learning? When have you had time for that if you're busy with all of this?"

Moshe Chaim sat speechless. He had no idea what to answer his father.

"It's the band, isn't it?" Mr. Kramer asked gently. "You've been concentrating on it so much that you seem to have forgotten all about your learning. Rabbi Goldsmith called me this afternoon, and he told me you have not been learning as well as you could lately. He suspected that your sudden lack of attention to your studies might have something to do with your band. After seeing all these signs in your room, I tend to agree with him. You've obviously been spending too much time working on your band projects instead of reviewing your learning."

Moshe Chaim nodded shamefacedly. It was clear to him now how much time all these extra band projects were taking up. Of course, his learning had suffered, though he hadn't realized why until now.

"In order to make your learning improve, I don't

think I have any other alternative but to make you leave the band."

"Leave the band?"

The words hit Moshe Chaim like a ton of bricks. How could he leave the band? The *Hachnassas Sefer Torah* was only a week away. How could he miss that? He had put in so much work already, with after school practices and the signs he had made.

"Please," he pleaded. "Anything but that. From now on, I'll work harder. I'll spend every second learning. I won't even think of the band."

"I'm sorry, Moshe Chaim. My mind is made up, and the answer is no."

Moshe Chaim couldn't believe it. How could he tell his friends that he would not be in the band? Where in the world would they find another drummer to take his place?

"I'm sorry, Moshe Chaim," his father continued, "but this can't go on. Your going to have to learn that your learning is much more important than playing drums."

"Please," he begged. "Next week is the *Hachnassas Sefer Torah*, and the guys need me to play with them. Punish me any other way you like, but don't make me leave the band just now."

Mr. Kramer shook his head, "I'm sorry, Moshe Chaim," he said sternly, "but I'm afraid that this is the only way you will learn to be more careful with your learning time in the future."

Moshe Chaim fought bravely to hold back the tears welling up in his eyes.

"Please?" he begged once again.

"I'm sorry, Moshe Chaim, but my mind is made up. I'm going to have to call your grandfather and tell him you won't be playing for his *shul's* function. I would advise you to call your friends in the band right away, so they can try and find someone to replace you."

Moshe Chaim thought back to his conversation with his grandfather two days earlier. He remembered how proud his grandfather had been of his learning and his musical talents. What would he think now?

"Oh no!" he cried. "Please don't tell Zeidie just yet. He'll be so disappointed in me."

Mr. Kramer looked down at his son. Moshe Chaim was bent over, as if he had a great pain in his stomach. His mouth was twisted in a frown, and a shiny little teardrop was beginning to find its way out of the corner of his eye.

"All right," he sighed. "I won't tell your grandfather. He'll find out soon enough anyway when he sees someone else playing the drums at the *Hachnassas Sefer Torah*."

Moshe Chaim knew his father was right, but he was grateful anyway. At least he would have another week before his grandfather found out the bad news.

"Thank you," he whispered.

"Okay," said Mr. Kramer, turning towards the door. "I'm going to go downstairs and tell your mother now. I'll also ask her not to tell your grandfather. Good night, Moshe Chaim. I'm sorry that I have to be so hard on you, but I really want you to learn your lesson."

"Good night," Moshe Chaim whispered in return.

Let's Do It Again!

When the door had closed, Moshe Chaim slowly lifted himself off the floor and threw himself down on his bed.

What was he going to do now?

How could he tell his friends that he wasn't allowed to be in the band any more? The *Hachnassas Sefer Torah* was only one week away. Where in the world would the guys find another drummer in time? He didn't know anyone else in his school who could play the drums. And how could he tell his friends that he hadn't been learning at all for the past week? He was so ashamed of himself that he felt like crying.

He just couldn't tell them.

That's it! he thought to himself. I won't tell them. There's still another week left before the *Hachnassas Sefer Torah*. Maybe I'll be able to find a solution to this problem by then. Until then, I'll just have to avoid coming to practice somehow.

Suddenly, a new thought occurred to him. Uh oh. I forgot that we're all supposed to go clean Reb Velvel's store tomorrow night. He's so nice to let us use his second-hand music store for our band practices. It's the least we can do to clean it up for him, but that's band business, and I'm not allowed to go. How will I explain to the boys when I don't show up for that as well? I'll have to think about it tomorrow, I guess.

The next day, a very sad looking Moshe Chaim showed up to school.

"Hey, Moshe Chaim," called Gavriel. "What's the matter? You look terrible!"

"Oh . . . I do?" asked Moshe Chaim. "I guess I must

be tired. I had a hard time falling asleep last night."

"I bet you couldn't fall asleep because you were thinking about the band."

"That's right," answered Moshe Chaim with a sigh. "I was thinking about the band."

"I have the same problem," said Gavriel. "I keep thinking about what songs we'll sing and what we'll wear. Do you think we should all wear matching ties?"

"That sounds nice," sighed Moshe Chaim.

He tried his best to look as happy as Gavriel, but it wasn't easy. Every time he spoke about the band, he felt a pain of sadness in his heart, but he just couldn't let Gavriel know what had happened.

"Did you hear about the new kind of pizza they started serving in the pizza shop?" asked Moshe Chaim, trying very hard to change the topic of conversation.

Class began with Rabbi Goldsmith passing back the quizzes. When he stopped at Moshe Chaim's desk, Moshe Chaim tried to avoid his *rebbi's* gaze. He couldn't miss, though, the look Rabbi Goldsmith gave him before he passed onto the next desk. He looked down at his paper and read the red ink on the top. "Please see me during recess."

Although he tried to pay attention for the rest of class, Moshe Chaim's eyes couldn't stop darting toward the clock on the wall. Usually, time went very slowly when he was in school. Many was the time that Moshe Chaim found himself wondering if the hands on the clock were stuck in one place. Today, however, when Moshe Chaim *wanted* the clock to move slowly,

68

it seemed to be moving faster than a rocket.

Moshe Chaim glanced at the clock once more. In only ten minutes, it would be time for recess. While all the other boys would run out to play, he would have to remain behind and face his *rebbi*.

It was not that he didn't like Rabbi Goldsmith. Moshe Chaim actually liked his *rebbi* a lot. When Rabbi Goldsmith taught something, he tried very hard to make sure that every boy in the class understood it. He almost never got angry during class.

Right now, however, Moshe Chaim couldn't help but remember the look he had gotten from Rabbi Goldsmith when he had passed back the quizzes.

All too soon, the bell rang. While all the other boys left the room to go to recess, Moshe Chaim remained behind in his seat, his heart pounding in his chest.

Rabbi Goldsmith walked over to Moshe Chaim's chair.

"Moshe Chaim," he said softly, "what's going on? You have always been a hard-working student. Now it seems to me that you have stopped *chazzering* and paying attention as much as you used to.

"You see," Rabbi Goldsmith continued, "I don't mind if a boy doesn't understand something in class, because not all boys can learn as fast as others. You, however, Moshe Chaim, have *b'li ayin hara* a very good head, and I expect you to be able to answer the type of questions that I've asked you."

Moshe Chaim found himself wishing that he was anywhere in the world except his classroom.

"Please, Moshe Chaim," said his *rebbi*, "try to spend

more time reviewing what we've learned in class, okay?"

"Yes," answered Moshe Chaim quietly.

"Good, I'm glad to hear that you're going to try harder. You may join the rest of the boys in the yard for the rest of recess."

"Thank you."

At recess, Moshe Chaim heard his friends speak of nothing else but the band, and he constantly found himself trying to change the subject.

Finally, school was over. All the boys quickly filed out of class.

"Moshe Chaim!" cried Gavriel. "Come on, we've all got to go clean Reb Velvel's store. That's our deal, remember? We have to finish quickly so we'll have enough time for another band practice afterwards."

"Yeah," answered Moshe Chaim. "I remember the deal, but I need to stop off at home first. You guys just go ahead without me. I can always catch up later."

"Okay," answered Gavriel. "I guess we'll see you soon."

Moshe Chaim didn't reply. He simply turned towards his house, while the other boys walked towards Reb Velvel's store.

"Gavriel," began Shaya as they walked down the street, "did you notice anything strange about Moshe Chaim today?"

"Yes, I did," answered Gavriel. "He seemed to be acting really weird the whole day. It looked like he was pretty upset about something. In fact, this is the first time that I ever remember seeing Moshe Chaim's freckled face without a smile on it. I'll bet it has to do with the band."

"Why do you say that?" asked Shaya.

"Because I noticed that every time we spoke about the band he would try and change the subject."

"Oh yeah," exclaimed Shaya, "I noticed that, too. When I wanted to talk to him about our songs, he only wanted to talk about the new neighbors on his block."

"He spoke to me about pizza," chuckled Gavriel.

"I was thinking that it might have to do with something that Rebbi said to him during recess," said Shaya.

"You're right," said Gavriel. "He looked pretty upset after he got that surprise quiz back from Rebbi. I bet that had something to do with why Rebbi wanted to see him during recess."

"So," began Binyamin, "what is bothering him, guys? Is it something about the band, or something about his learning?"

"I wonder," said Gavriel. "Maybe it has something to do with both."

"What do you mean?" asked Shaya as they approached the door to Reb Velvel's store.

The conversation was interrupted by the chimes on the door which rang as they walked inside.

"Ah," cried Reb Velvel, "Gavriel and Shaya, Binyamin and Yossi, it's so good to see you! Welcome! Welcome! What a pleasure it is to have such wonderful company. Your bright, young faces always make me feel so happy."

Even though they were still upset about Moshe

Chaim's behavior, the boys couldn't help but smile when they saw Reb Velvel's cheerful face.

"I heard that you're going to be playing at the *Hachnassas Sefer Torah* next week."

"Yes," said Gavriel, "we really can't wait until then. We've got to practice every minute that we have now."

"But," added Shaya, "we're going to clean anyway because of the deal we made with you before *Lag Baomer.*"

"Such wonderful boys!" Reb Velvel cried. "They're so busy preparing with so little time to practice, but they come to clean anyway. Such diamonds! No matter what, they always keep their word. What pure and holy boys they are, *mamish* young *tzaddikim.*"

"Where should we start cleaning first?" asked Gavriel, a little embarrassed at all the praise.

"Well," Reb Velvel said, holding two feather dusters, "maybe you and Binyamin could dust the instruments while Shaya and Yossi sweep the floor. I'm going to go to the back of the store to get something right now. Just call me if you need me."

"Okay," the boys called as they watched the hunched figure with the short white beard disappear into the back rooms of the store. With every step that he took, he sang a tune with his favorite words, chirry bim chirry bum.

"He's such a nice man," sighed Shaya.

"That's for sure," Binyamin agreed. "I like being with him, because he's always happy. It's hard to feel sad around someone who's so happy all the time."

"Yeah," said Gavriel, "when he was in the room I

forgot all about Moshe Chaim and whatever is bothering him."

"What were you saying before about Moshe Chaim being upset about both the band and his learning?"

"Well," said Gavriel, "I've been thinking that maybe the reason Moshe Chaim looked so upset when he got the quiz back is because he hasn't been paying attention in class. Maybe he's been too busy thinking about the band. I know that my own *yetzer hara* keeps telling me to do that during class."

"Hmm," said Shaya, taking his first sweep with the broom, "that could be. Maybe Moshe Chaim has been thinking about the band too much, and maybe he's been spending too much time making band posters instead of reviewing his learning."

"What are you guys talking about?" interrupted Binyamin. "Why should Moshe Chaim's learning be affected by the band? I don't think my learning has been."

"What do you mean?" asked Gavriel. "Don't you feel like thinking about the band during class?"

"Yes, I do," answered Binyamin. "But what's wrong with doing a little thinking about the band in between learning anyway?"

"Yeah," Yossi agreed, as he swept a pile of dust into a dustpan, "I guess it's like taking a break."

"That's right," said Binyamin, trying very hard to reach the top of a hanging violin with his feather duster. "My *rebbi* gives us recess every day. He says it's so we can come back to our learning feeling refreshed and strong. Taking a little break to think about the band makes me feel refreshed."

"That's in between learning," said Shaya. "But what about thinking about the band during learning?"

"Yeah," said Gavriel, "how can you pay attention to what your *rebbi* is saying when you're thinking about something else?"

"I can do that," answered Binyamin with confidence.

"I think I'll clean these bagpipes," Gavriel said. "They look a little dusty."

"Hey," Shaya cried, "maybe I could play that instead of my clarinet. That thing should make the band sound really interesting."

"Are you kidding?" laughed Gavriel. "They sound terrible. Besides you couldn't play them anyway. They're almost as big as you are."

"That's true!" Shaya chuckled.

"What about these things?" asked Yossi while taking a few thumps on a bongo drum. "Maybe Moshe Chaim could play them instead of his regular drums. I'm sure that would look pretty funny."

"Where is Moshe Chaim, anyway?" asked Gavriel.

"Hey," cried Binyamin, "you're right. Moshe Chaim should have been here by now." He paused to dust the top of an accordion. "It shouldn't take that long for him to go to his house and come back here."

"I'll bet," said Gavriel, "that he's walking slowly, because he's so upset that his learning has been affected by the band."

"I still say," said Binyamin, "that thinking about the band shouldn't affect his learning at all."

Let's Do It Again!

Suddenly, Reb Velvel walked back into the room.

"Hey," Shaya whispered, "I've got a great idea. Why don't we ask Reb Velvel what he thinks?"

"That's a good idea," Gavriel agreed.

"Is everything okay, boys?" Reb Velvel asked as the boys approached him.

"Yes," Shaya answered. "We've finished cleaning, but we have something we need to ask you."

"We need your advice," Gavriel said.

"My advice?" asked Reb Velvel in surprise. "For advice you should go to a parent or a *rebbi*. I am just a plain, old storekeeper. What kind of advice can I offer?"

"Well," Gavriel said, "our problem has something to do with our band, and you've given our band a lot of good advice in the past."

"What is this problem?" asked Reb Velvel.

"You see," Shaya began, "as you know, we are supposed to play at the *Hachnassas Sefer Torah* next week."

"And," continued Gavriel, "we noticed that Moshe Chaim Kramer was very upset today. Shaya and I think that he's upset because he didn't know the answers to a quiz on the *Gemara* yesterday. We think that his thinking too much about the band might be affecting his learning."

"But," said Binyamin, "Yossi and I feel that doing a little thinking about the band couldn't be interfering with his learning that much."

"Hmm," Reb Velvel said, stroking his short white beard. "I see your point. You feel that it's not so hard

75

to think about your band and listen to your *rebbi* at the same time."

"That's right," said Yossi.

"Hmm," said Reb Velvel, stroking his beard some more, "did you talk about the band while you were cleaning here today?"

"A little," Gavriel answered, "but what does that have to do with anything?"

"I'm no big *talmid chacham*," Reb Velvel said modestly. "Like I said before, I'm just a plain, old storekeeper."

The boys remained silent.

"But," Reb Velvel continued, "I do know someone who knows the answer to your problem."

"Who?" all the boys asked eagerly.

"Why, you boys, of course," Reb Velvel cried.

"What do you mean?" Shaya asked. "We asked you, because we weren't sure ourselves."

"Do you boys think that you did a good job cleaning today?" Reb Velvel asked.

"Yes," the confused boys answered. "We spent almost an hour doing it."

"Do you think that you cleaned just as well as you've been learning?"

"I guess so," Gavriel answered.

"Well," said Reb Velvel with a big smile, "to find out how well you can learn while thinking about something else, I think you should check to see how well you cleaned while you were talking about something else. To see how well you can do two things at once, all you have to do is check around the store and see if you missed any dust or dirt."

"What do you mean?" asked Yossi.

Reb Velvel looked at the boys over the rims of his black spectacles and continued. "If you cleaned as well as you say you learned, then you shouldn't find any dust at all."

"Hey," Gavriel cried, "that's right!"

"So," Shaya said, "what are we waiting for? Let's check for dust."

"Where should we start?" Binyamin asked Gavriel.

"Let's check those violins you cleaned first. We were talking about the band a little when you did them."

"Okay," said Binyamin. "Here's a chair. I'll climb up and check them for dust."

Binyamin pulled his chair up to the third violin.

"I remember cleaning this one," he said. "I'm sure there isn't a speck of dust on it."

Binyamin ran his fingers across the curved wood on top of the instrument and then held up his fingers for all to see.

"It looks like there was a little more than a speck of dust left up there," Shaya chuckled upon seeing Binyamin's black, dust-covered fingers.

"I don't understand!" Binyamin cried. "I was sure I cleaned just great."

"Maybe you accidentally missed that violin," Gavriel suggested. "Try checking the next one."

"Yeah," Binyamin agreed, "that's a good idea. Maybe I forgot to clean this one. Here, let me check the next violin."

Binyamin ran the fingers of his other hand across

the top of the next violin.

"You see," he said, triumphantly holding up his fingers, "not a speck of dust. I told you I cleaned real good."

"I don't know," Shaya said. "That violin doesn't really look very clean. Try checking the sides of it for dust."

"Okay," agreed Binyamin, sliding his fingers down the smooth sides of the instrument. "You'll see. There won't be a speck of dust here either."

"Then what's that black stuff on your hand?" Yossi laughed.

Binyamin ran his hand along the top and sides of each instrument and was shocked to find that none of them was perfectly clean.

"I just don't understand it," he cried.

"Now let's check the floor where I swept," said Yossi. "I'm sure we won't find any dirt there."

"Oh no?" laughed Gavriel. "What's this piece of paper over here?"

"That's funny," said Yossi. "I didn't see it there before."

"What about this pile of dust in the corner?" asked Gavriel, pointing to the floor once again.

"I know I swept that part of the floor before," cried Yossi. "Maybe the wind blew that dirt there."

"What wind?" Gavriel asked. "The door hasn't been opened once since we came in."

"You're right," Yossi agreed. "I just don't understand it."

"Do you think Reb Velvel was right?" Binyamin

asked. "Do you think we did a bad job cleaning because we were talking about the band?"

"It must be," answered Yossi. "I'm going to be a lot more careful about my paying attention in class from now on."

"I think we all will," agreed Gavriel picking up his feather duster. "Right now, I think we'd better clean this place again, and no talking this time. Right?"

"Right!" agreed his friends.

The boys cleaned like they had never cleaned before, and not one word was uttered the whole time. A cloud of dust soon filled the air.

"What is going on, boys?" asked Reb Velvel, coughing. "I thought you finished cleaning already?"

"We also thought we finished," Gavriel answered, "but we realized that we were wrong. This time we really want to make the place spotless."

"That's very good, boys," Reb Velvel said with a smile. "Just don't work too hard."

He walked away, with a new chirry bim tune on his lips.

Finally, the job was done.

"This time, this store is really clean!" Gavriel cried as he put down his feather duster. "I think we even have time for one quick practice of all the songs we picked yesterday."

"Good night, Reb Velvel!" the boys called later as they walked out the door. "Thank you very much for all your help."

"My help?" Reb Velvel asked. "Ahh, such diamonds these boys are. They come and clean up for an old man, and they thank him for his help? *Mamish* wonderful, young men."

"Good-bye, Reb Velvel."

"Good-bye, boys."

The chimes rang as the front door closed.

"Hey," cried Shaya as they walked out onto the street, "Moshe Chaim never showed up at all."

"Yeah," agreed Gavriel, "that's really weird. I'll try to call him as soon as I get home to find out what's going on."

CHAPTER

FIVE

Little Sisters

Gavriel couldn't wait to speak to Moshe Chaim and find out what was going on. Unfortunately, he had no time to call before supper began.

"What do you think I should do, Mommy?" he asked his mother at the dinner table. "Something is obviously bothering Moshe Chaim very much. He didn't even show up at Reb Velvel's store tonight to help us clean. Should I call him right now and find out why?"

"I don't know, Gavriel," Mrs. Weintraub answered. "Often, when a person has a problem the best thing to do is speak about it with a friend, because he might be able to help. Why don't you wait until tomorrow morning and have a talk with Moshe Chaim in school? He might feel more comfortable talking to you in person than on the phone."

"Okay," answered Gavriel. "I'll try to do that."

"Hey, Gavriel," said Binyamin, with a big smile on his face. "Guess what tonight is."

"What?" asked Gavriel.

"Tonight is the night you get to do the dishes."

"Oh no!" moaned Gavriel. "I hate doing the dishes."

"Don't worry, Gavriel," said his little sister Dassie. "I'll help you."

Gavriel turned to his little sister. "I'll wash, and you dry. Okay, Dassie?"

"That's no fair," Dassie complained. "I never get to wash! Let me do the washing today, Gavriel."

"You can't even reach the sink."

"I can if I stand on this chair," answered Dassie, pushing a kitchen chair towards the sink.

"Okay, Dassie," Gavriel said. "You can do the washing if you really think you can."

"I know I can," said Dassie, full of confidence.

"Okay," said Gavriel. "So start washing. I'll be back in a few minutes. That way you'll have a chance to get a head start on the dishes."

As Gavriel left the kitchen, he heard the water beginning to pour out of the faucet.

I guess Dassie isn't a baby any more, he thought to himself. Nowadays, she wants to do everything that Binyamin and I do. She always sees us washing the dishes, and now she wants to do it, too, not that we mind, of course. One day, she'll be able to do the washing and the drying. Maybe she'll like it so much that Binyamin and I will never have to do the dishes.

"How's the washing coming along?" he shouted from the other room.

Let's Do It Again!

"They're almost all clean already," Dassie answered proudly.

Boy, that was fast, Gavriel thought to himself with a smile as he jogged towards the kitchen. I'd better hurry up and start drying those dishes.

As soon as he entered the kitchen, the smile on Gavriel's face turned into a look of horror.

Water was pouring out of the kitchen sink at full blast, and Dassie was holding the plate right up to the faucet. The water splashed right off the plate and splattered all over the kitchen.

Little streams of water poured down the door of the refrigerator. The curtains on the window were completely soaked. Even the ceiling was wet.

Gavriel looked down, and to his great horror, he saw that his shoes were under water.

"Dassie!" he cried. "Turn off the water! Hurry!"

Dassie quickly turned to face her brother, causing the water to splash directly in Gavriel's face.

"What's the matter, Gavriel?" she asked. "Why do you want me to turn off the sink? I'm washing the dishes really good."

"You're not just washing the dishes," Gavriel spluttered as he reached over to turn off the faucet. "You're washing the whole room."

Suddenly, Gavriel heard a scream from behind him.

"Uh oh," Gavriel moaned. "That sounded like Mommy. We're really in trouble now, Dassie."

"My kitchen!" Mrs. Weintraub cried. "What have you done to my kitchen?"

"Gavriel and I are washing the dishes," Dassie said proudly.

Mrs. Weintraub turned to her son.

"Gavriel," she cried, "are you responsible for this?"

"All I did was let Dassie wash the dishes," Gavriel stammered. "I just walked out for a minute."

"You know that Dassie is too young to wash the dishes by herself."

"I'm sorry," Gavriel answered. "I guess I should have realized that."

"What's the matter, Mommy?" Dassie asked. "Didn't I do a good job cleaning?"

"You cleaned a little too good," her mother answered. "My entire kitchen is under water."

Dassie looked down and noticed the flood on the floor for the first time.

"Uh oh," she squeaked.

"Okay, you two," said Mrs. Weintraub trying very hard to remain calm. "I want you both to put your rubbers on, get out some towels and a mop and start wiping up this mess. Do you understand me?"

"Yes, Mommy," they both answered.

"Good. Now get to work."

Gavriel glared at his sister. "Now look what you did," he cried. "It'll probably take half an hour to clean up this mess."

Dassie didn't seem to hear her brother. She just grabbed a towel, put it down on the floor and started to sing a song.

"Could you stop singing and help me at least?" asked a very angry Gavriel.

Let's Do It Again!

"I'm gonna help you," answered Dassie. "You'll see."

Gavriel looked on in amazement as Dassie grabbed three towels, threw them onto the water and began to do a dance on top of them.

"What are you doing?" he yelled.

"I'm wiping," she answered. "I'm allowed to wipe with my feet. What makes you think you can yell at me anyway?"

"What is that supposed to mean?" Gavriel asked angrily. "I certainly didn't make this mess. Why should I have to clean it up anyway?"

"Who told you to leave me alone?" Dassie asked innocently. "And stop yelling at me, or I'm going to tell Mommy."

"Oh, I give up," Gavriel grumbled as he began to wipe. "Little sisters can drive you crazy."

It took a long time, but after a lot of mopping and wringing and grumbling from Gavriel, the room was finally dried.

When the last towel was wrung and hung to dry, he glanced up at the clock on the kitchen wall. It was ten to eight, and he would have to leave to Shaya's house now for their nightly study session. At least he wouldn't have a little sister there to bother him.

Gavriel woke up and dressed quickly the next morning. He was anxious to get to school and speak to Moshe Chaim. He just had to find out what was bothering him and why he had not shown up to clean the night before.

"What's the matter, Gavriel?" Binyamin asked as

85

he watched his brother bend over to tie his shoe.

"What's the matter," answered Gavriel, "is that our little sister made me spend the whole night mopping the kitchen, and now my neck is a little stiff."

"Yeah," chuckled Binyamin, "that Dassie can sure be a pain in the neck sometimes."

"Ha, ha, ha," grumbled Gavriel. "Very funny."

"Anyway," said Binyamin, "we'd better start walking to *yeshivah*."

Gavriel had wanted to speak to Moshe Chaim before class started. Unfortunately, Moshe Chaim did not enter the room until class was about to begin.

Gavriel looked at his friend and couldn't believe his eyes. Moshe Chaim had one arm in a sling and was walking with a limp. What on earth had happened to him?

When it was time for recess, the boys swarmed out the door. Gavriel and Shaya waited to see if Moshe Chaim needed any help.

"What happened to you?" asked Shaya as they headed outside together.

"Is this why you didn't come to Reb Velvel's store last night?" asked Gavriel as he held the door open for Moshe Chaim to go outside.

"Yes," answered Moshe Chaim sadly, limping over to the big tree beside the playground.

He leaned against the trunk, trying to appear casual.

Gavriel eyed him suspiciously. Something just wasn't right with the way Moshe Chaim was acting.

"You see," Moshe Chaim explained, "after we left

school yesterday, I ran home to get something. I was in such a hurry that I didn't look where I was going. When I walked into my room, I stepped on a roller skate, slipped and flew straight into the wall. I think I sprained my wrist, not to mention whatever it is that I did to my leg."

Moshe Chaim lifted his pants leg to reveal an ace bandage which was wrapped around his knee. It seemed to Gavriel that Moshe Chaim had another reason to bend over at that moment as well. During his whole speech, Moshe Chaim had appeared quite uncomfortable. He hadn't even been able to look either boy in the eye. Could Moshe Chaim have concocted the whole story? Even if he had, the question was, why? What was Moshe Chaim hiding? Gavriel was determined now more than ever to find out what was wrong with his friend.

"I guess this means you won't be playing any punchball today," said Gavriel pointedly.

"Yeah." Moshe Chaim laughed nervously. "Not to mention playing the drums for the *Hachnassas Sefer Torah.*"

"What do you mean?" demanded Shaya. "Your wrist will certainly be better by then. It has to be. If you can't play the drums, what's going to be with the band? You know how important a drummer is. How long do you think you'll have to wear that anyway?"

Gavriel rolled his eyes. The whole scene seemed too fishy.

Moshe Chaim just shrugged his shoulders.

What a stroke of luck he had had the night before.

The Cheery Bim Band

When he had come home from school, he had been in a panic, trying frantically to come up with some excuse as to why he could not join his friends at Reb Velvel's store. When he walked into his room, he really did slip on a roller skate, and he actually had crashed into the wall. There had only been one problem. He had not been hurt at all. That didn't stop him though. Moshe Chaim then spent half an hour searching through his drawers, looking for the old ace bandage and sling. He was glad that he had saved them from the time he had fallen from a tree in third grade. Now he had the perfect excuse, without really having to lie. All he had to do was make believe he was in pain.

The only problem was that he was having a hard time remembering which foot he was supposed to be limping on.

Gavriel wanted to have his talk with Moshe Chaim, but by now the other boys had spotted Moshe Chaim and had all come over to find out what had happened. Their talk would have to wait until after school.

When classes ended, Gavriel went to the front of the classroom to wish his *rebbi* a good *Shabbos*, and then he ran down the stairs to catch Moshe Chaim and walk him home.

When he got to the front of the building he looked down the block and was amazed to find that Moshe Chaim was nowhere in sight. How could he have disappeared so fast with all those injuries? It didn't seem possible.

Oh well, thought Gavriel, my talk with Moshe Chaim will have to wait until after *Shabbos*. I guess I'll head home myself. Maybe I'll have time to call Shaya and speak to him before *Shabbos*.

"Gavriel!" came a shout as he walked into the house. His sister Dassie nearly knocked him to the floor as she came running at him, leaping into his arms.

"Hello, Dassie," he managed as he tried to regain his balance.

He untangled himself from Dassie's loving embrace only to find himself covered with what appeared to be chocolate handprints in every place Dassie had hugged him.

"What's all this?" he asked, trying to remain calm as he felt himself growing angry again at his little sister.

"I was helping Mommy clean for *Shabbos*," she answered.

"That's very good, Dassie. Preparing for *Shabbos* is a very big *mitzvah*, but what's this stuff all over us? Not from cleaning the house I assume?"

Dassie looked at the sticky brown handprints on her brother's clothes in surprise.

"Oh that. I got tired of cleaning, so I decided to bake a cake."

"A cake?" Gavriel spluttered. "Since when do you know how to bake cakes?"

"It was easy," declared the six-year-old. "Do you want to see it?"

"No, I don't want to see it," Gavriel answered, pushing past her. "On second thought, maybe I better see this cake. I hope it looks better than I do."

Dassie trotted along after him into the kitchen.

"Dassie!" Gavriel exploded when he saw the mess in the kitchen. "What did you do?"

"I made a cake!" Dassie answered, proudly pointing to a strange-looking brown glob of dough on the kitchen table.

"Look at this mess!" he cried. "It'll take half an hour just to clean it up. There's flour all over the floor, dough all over the chairs and chocolate pudding all over the table. I even see some sprinkles stuck to the ceiling. Mommy wants this place all clean for *Shabbos*, not messy like this. Now I'll never have time to call Shaya before *Shabbos*."

"Why are you yelling at me again? Stop it right now, or I'm going to tell Mommy."

"Oh yeah? Be my guest, but don't blame me this time when you get into trouble. Wait till she sees this mess!"

Dassie began to look worried. "Gavriel," she wheedled, "maybe you'll help me clean this up. Then I won't tell Mommy that you yelled at me."

Gavriel glared at his little sister. It wouldn't do, though, to get his mother upset. He began to wipe up the table. When he got to the mess in the middle, he simply pulled over the garbage can and pushed it all inside.

"That was my cake," screamed Dassie. "I wanted everyone to have it for *Shabbos*. Why did you do that anyway?"

"Because no one would even touch such a cake, Dassie," Gavriel yelled back. "Why don't you just be quiet and clean up?"

"Because I don't wanna be quiet, and besides, you're wrong. Everyone would have loved my cake."

"They would not!"

"Would too!"

"Would not!"

"Would too!"

"Would not!"

Dassie began to wipe the floor, purposefully ignoring Gavriel.

"Great, just great," Gavriel mumbled to himself. "First, I have to mop up her mess when she washes the dishes, and now I have to clean up her mess when she bakes a cake. Little sisters! What a pain in the neck!"

Finally, the house was cleaned, and the entire Weintraub family was ready for *Shabbos*.

The whole family gathered around the dining room table, as Mrs. Weintraub lit the candles atop her shining silver candelabra.

Mr. Weintraub and his sons wore their finest suits, while his two daughters Miriam and Dassie wore their nicest dresses. The house was spotless; it seemed to glow with cleanliness.

Mrs. Weintraub finished saying her *brachah* over the candles. The whole family wished each other a good *Shabbos*, and all the men left to *shul*.

Gavriel took a deep breath of the sweet spring air. Ahh, how he loved *Shabbos*!

Soon, they arrived at the *shul*. Gavriel and Binyamin sat on either side of their father.

The boys loved to *daven* along with the *chazan*, and they especially loved to sing *Lecha Dodi*. Over and over, they sang the song welcoming the *Shabbos* bride.

When *davening* was over, everyone shook hands and wished each other a good *Shabbos* before walking home.

At home, it was once again time for singing. This time, they welcomed the *Shabbos* angels. *"Shalom Aleichem, Malachei Hashareis . . ."*

The purple wine stood ready in the crystal decanter. The fresh *challos* sat under their cover. Everything looked just beautiful. This house certainly was prepared nicely to greet *Shabbos.*

Mr. Weintraub lifted his silver *becher* and made *Kiddush.* Then, after everyone had washed their hands, he lifted the two golden *challos* and made *Hamotzi.*

The fish was served, and then it was time to begin the Weintraubs' favorite part of the *Shabbos* meal, the singing of *zemiros.*

All weekday problems were quickly forgotten, as Mr. Weintraub began to sing, *"Kah Ribon Olam Ve'almaya . . ."*

Gavriel and Binyamin looked at each other, winked and joined in the singing, their sweet high-pitched voices creating a nice contrast to the deep voice of their father.

"Ant Hoo Malka Melech Malchaya . . ."

Over and over, they sang, and each beautiful word seemed to hang in the air like a crystal chandelier.

All too soon, however, it was time for the singing to stop and the soup to be served.

"Can I please have some more soup, Mommy?" asked Binyamin. He then turned to his sister Miriam.

"You see, Miriam, I said please, your favorite word."

Miriam was a teacher in the Riverport Beis Yaakov, and was always trying to teach her brothers the same good *midos* she taught in school.

"Yes," she answered, "but you didn't say thank you when Mommy gave you your fish."

"*Oy,*" Binyamin groaned. "I knew she would find something wrong."

Everyone chuckled.

"Mommy," began Gavriel, "do we have any red ties?"

"Why do you want a red tie?" asked Mrs. Weintraub. "Are you afraid that someone is going to give you an *ayin hara,* or are you going somewhere important tonight?"

"No, Mommy," Binyamin mumbled through a mouthful of chicken. "He wants to wear it to the *Hachnassas Sefer Torah* next week."

"Binyamin!" Miriam cried. "Don't talk with your mouth full!"

"But I don't have time to talk in between the bites," Binyamin complained.

"Then don't talk at all," his mother answered. "Now, what's this about a red tie, Gavriel?"

"Well," he said first gulping down what was in his mouth, "since we will all be wearing suits to the *Hachnassas Sefer Torah,* we were thinking that maybe all the members of the band could wear matching red ties."

"That sounds very nice," Mrs. Weintraub said, "but I'm not sure we have any red ties. I'll have to check after *Shabbos.*"

"So, I see that you boys are all excited about playing next week," said Mr. Weintraub.

"We sure are," answered Binyamin. "We can't wait until Thursday. We still have a lot of practicing to do on all the songs we're going to be playing."

"I hope you guys play *Samcheim,* like you did at the *Lag Baomer* street fair," said Miriam.

"I know that song," shouted Dassie. "*Oy Yoy Yoy Yoy . . .*"

"Stop singing!" cried Gavriel. "I'm in the middle of talking now."

"No!" answered Dassie. "I don't want to. Mommy, Gavriel's yelling at me."

"Gavriel," said Mr. Weintraub, "why are you yelling at your sister?"

"Because she's such a pain in the neck."

"Gavriel," cried Mrs. Weintraub, "that's not very nice."

"Well," answered Gavriel, "I didn't think that it was very nice when she flooded the kitchen, and I had to wipe it all up. I also didn't think it was very nice of her to make a mess in the kitchen before *Shabbos,* that I also had to clean up. And now she's sitting there interrupting me when I talk. Why does she think she can walk all over me?"

The room suddenly grew very quiet. Everyone was shocked at the way Gavriel was acting. Everyone except for Dassie. She was also angry.

"He yells at me every day!" she cried, pointing her finger at her brother. "I was only trying to help him do the dishes and bake a cake."

Let's Do It Again!

"Uh oh," Mr. Weintraub whispered to his wife, "I think we have a fight on our hands."

He turned to the children.

"Gavriel, Dassie, I'm ashamed of both of you. How could you spoil our quiet peaceful *Shabbos seudah* by fighting? Don't you know that the *Beis Hamikdash* was destroyed because our people were fighting with each other?"

Gavriel glared at Dassie, and Dassie glared right back at him. This fight was definitely not over.

The next morning, things were not much better. Gavriel woke up late and was in a hurry to get to *shul*.

"Where's my tie?" he cried, as he walked into the kitchen. "I left it on the couch last night, and now it's not there any more."

"Well, Gavriel," said his mother, "you should know better than to leave your clothing lying around the living room. Maybe this will teach you a lesson."

"But I'm late for *shul*, Mommy," he moaned.

"Okay," she sighed. "I'll help you look for it."

"Did you see it, Miriam?" Gavriel asked his older sister.

"The last time I saw it was when Dassie was straightening up the living room last night."

Aha, thought Gavriel. Dassie must have put it somewhere.

"Dassie!" he yelled. "Where are you?"

"I'm right here," came a small voice from behind Gavriel.

"Did you put my tie anywhere?" he asked.

"Yes," answered Dassie. "I cleaned up the living

room last night, and I put it away with everything else that I found there."

"So, where is it?" asked Gavriel anxiously. "I'm late for *shul*."

"It's in the coat closet," she answered.

"In the coat closet?" cried Gavriel. "Why in the world did you put it in the coat closet? How did you ever expect me to find it there?"

"When you take out your coat you'll find it," Dassie answered.

"Dassie," cried Gavriel, "it's sixty-five degrees outside. I'm not going to wear a coat."

"Well, I didn't know that," said Dassie sheepishly.

"If I wouldn't have asked you, I probably wouldn't have found my tie until next winter."

"That would be funny," Dassie giggled.

"No it wouldn't be funny," cried Gavriel. "I would have spent the whole morning going crazy looking for that tie, and you think it's funny?"

"Yes, it's funny."

"Is not!"

"Is too!"

"Is not!"

"Is too!"

"Is not!"

"Mommy!" Dassie cried. "He's yelling at me again! Tell him to stop."

"Both of you, stop this fighting at once," cried Mrs. Weintraub. "Gavriel, you leave to *shul*, and Dassie, go put on your *Shabbos* dress."

"Yes, Mommy," they both answered.

Let's Do It Again!

By *shalosh seudos*, things weren't much better.

"Mommy!" Gavriel cried. "Dassie took the last *challah* roll. I had to use *matzah* instead. She knows that I need two *challah* rolls for *lechem mishneh*. Why'd she take it?"

"Because it was there," answered Dassie with a smile.

"You see what I mean," Gavriel cried. "Little sisters are a pain in the neck."

Later, after *Havdalah*, Gavriel decided to call Shaya.

"*Gut vach*, Shaya," he said into the phone when he heard his friend's voice.

"*Gut vach*, Gavriel," his friend answered. "What's up?"

"I really wanted to call you on Friday, but because of my pain-in-the-neck little sister I didn't get a chance to."

"Uh oh," said Shaya, "I have a feeling that you and Dassie did not exactly have a quiet, peaceful *Shabbos*."

"You're right," said Gavriel. "We didn't. Almost every second, my parents had to stop us from fighting."

"Boy," said Shaya, "that could be a problem."

"Speaking of problems," said Gavriel, "what did you think about the injuries Moshe Chaim told us about on Friday?"

"I thought it was very weird," answered Shaya. "Moshe Chaim didn't really look like he was in any pain at all."

"Well, I think I saw him limping on the wrong foot," Gavriel said. "Something really strange is going on."

"Yeah," agreed Shaya, "it looks to me like Moshe

Chaim is trying to hide something that is bothering him very much."

"I think that we should try to speak to him about it tomorrow," suggested Gavriel. "Maybe we can help him."

"Good idea!" agreed Shaya. "And speaking of good ideas, I think it would be a good idea for us to start working on our new song."

"Right now?" asked Gavriel.

"Why not? I've got a pen and paper on the table in front of me. Let's start working."

"Yeah, why not," agreed Gavriel.

"Since we will be playing two days before *Shavuos*, and since we will be celebrating the arrival of a new *Sefer Torah*, I think it would be a good idea to sing about Torah."

"How about we sing about how we got the Torah on Har Sinai?"

"Good idea," agreed Shaya. "Now what rhymes with Sinai?"

CHAPTER SIX

Missing Pieces

"How come you're in such a good mood today, Gavriel?" Binyamin asked his brother the next morning.

"Because," answered Gavriel, "Shaya and I spent a long time on the phone last night, and we made up a great new song for the band."

"Oh yeah?" cried Binyamin. "That's great. I can't wait to hear it."

"Actually," said Gavriel, "it's not really one song. We made up a whole bunch of different songs, and we want to call a band meeting to see which one to use. I have them all written up on a few sheets of paper."

"Hurry up, boys," called Mr. Weintraub from downstairs. "I don't want to be late for *davening*."

Mr. Weintraub was waiting as he always did on Sunday mornings, ready to walk his sons to *yeshivah*.

"Good morning," the boys greeted their father as they came down the stairs.

"Good morning, boys," he answered. "Are you ready to leave yet?"

"Yes," answered Gavriel, "just as soon as I get my *Gemara* and song sheets from the dining room table."

"Gavriel," said Mr. Weintraub, "your sister Dassie is sitting and playing quietly at the table. Please try not to get into any more fights with her, okay?"

"Okay, I'll try."

Gavriel walked into the dining room and found his little sister engrossed in a picture she was painting. Her water colors were on one side of her paper and a cup of muddy water on the other. The table in front of her was covered with works of art that she had set out to dry.

"Hello, Gavriel," Dassie cried when she saw her big brother. "Do you want to see all the pictures I just made?"

Gavriel smiled. Dassie seemed to have forgotten all about the arguments they had had the day before.

Well, he thought to himself, if she's willing to forget about our fighting, I guess I am, too.

"Good morning, Dassie," he answered cheerfully. "The pictures are beautiful, but I'm late, so I'm just going to find my *Gemara* somewhere under here and my song sheets, and leave for school."

Gavriel walked over to the table and found his *Gemara* under a few sodden water color paintings.

"Hey!" he cried after peering under all the papers on the table. "Where are my song sheets?"

Let's Do It Again!

"I don't know," answered Dassie. "They were there before."

"What did you do with them, Dassie?" he cried.

"I didn't take them," Dassie wailed. "And why are you yelling at me?"

"I don't want to yell at you, Dassie," he answered through gritted teeth. "Just tell me what you did with my song sheets. They're very important, and I have to leave for school now."

"Well, I didn't take them," answered a very annoyed Dassie.

"I don't believe you," answered Gavriel.

"I didn't," declared Dassie.

"Did too!" Gavriel answered angrily.

"Did not!"

"Did too!"

"Did not!"

"Did—"

Suddenly, Mr. Weintraub came racing into the room.

"What's going on in here?" he asked.

"Gavriel's fighting with me!" Dassie cried.

"Didn't I just ask you not to fight with your sister, Gavriel?"

"Yes, you did," answered Gavriel, "but I couldn't help it. Dassie took my song sheets, and they're really important. Shaya and I spent a long time working very hard to make up a few new songs. We have to pick which one we're going to sing on Thursday."

"I didn't take them!" cried Dassie.

"She did too!" answered Gavriel.

"Did not!"

"Did too!"

"Wait a minute," cried Mr. Weintraub. "This is not getting us anywhere. Dassie, did you take Gavriel's papers?"

"No," answered Dassie.

"Don't you believe your sister when she tells you something, Gavriel?" asked Mr. Weintraub.

"No!" answered Gavriel. "She told me that they were there before, and now they're gone. Things don't just disappear like that, you know, and she was the only one in this room all morning."

"Doesn't Shaya have a copy of the song sheets, too?" Mr. Weintraub asked, seeing he wasn't getting anywhere the other way.

"No!" answered Gavriel. "We made up the words over the phone, but I was the one who wrote them down."

"Well, don't you remember the words?"

"Not from all five songs," said Gavriel.

Suddenly, Mr. Weintraub looked at his watch.

"Oh my goodness!" he cried."We're late. We have to leave right now, or else we'll miss *Barchu*. Hurry!" And he quickly pulled Gavriel out of the room.

Later at recess, Gavriel told Shaya the bad news.

"Shaya," he began.

"Yes, Gavriel. What's up?"

"Well, do you remember those songs we spent so much time writing last night?"

"Of course, I remember them. They're all really

great songs. It'll probably be very hard to choose which one is the best."

"It might be even harder than you think," said Gavriel.

"Huh? . . . Why?"

"Because," answered Gavriel, "all the song sheets I wrote them on are gone."

"*What?*" Shaya yelled. "What do you mean, they're gone? We just made them up last night?"

"I know," Gavriel answered, "but when I woke up this morning they weren't on the table where I left them."

"Well, maybe somebody moved them somewhere else," suggested Shaya.

"No one we know of would have done that," came Binyamin's voice from behind Gavriel.

"No one," added Gavriel, "except for Dassie. We've been fighting so much lately. I'm sure she took them to get back at me even if she claims she didn't."

"I don't know," piped up Yossi Belsky. "We learned in *Pirkei Avos* that we're supposed to judge everyone favorably, even little sisters who drive you crazy."

"Hm," said Gavriel.

"Say," interrupted Shaya, "where's Moshe Chaim?"

"I don't know," answered Gavriel. "I don't remember him ever missing recess before."

"Maybe he doesn't want to come out, with all of those injuries," Binyamin suggested.

Suddenly, Gavriel let out a cry. "Oh no, I forgot to talk to Moshe Chaim and find out what's been bothering him."

"So," said Binyamin, "why don't you go talk to him now?"

"I think I will," said Gavriel, jogging back towards the school building. "I just hope there's enough time left to recess."

Gavriel found Moshe Chaim sitting all alone at his desk in their classroom. He looked very sad and lonely, sitting there bent over, wrapping and unwrapping his bandaged leg. Something was definitely on his mind, and Gavriel was determined to find out exactly what it was.

"Hi, Moshe Chaim," he called. "I thought you could use some company."

"Oh!" exclaimed a startled Moshe Chaim. "Hi, Gavriel. I didn't see you coming."

"How are you feeling?" Gavriel asked.

"*Baruch Hashem*, I feel better, thank you."

Gavriel sat down next to his friend.

Uh oh, thought Moshe Chaim to himself. He's looking at my sling. Does he know that I don't really need it?

His heart started beating quickly.

"Moshe Chaim," Gavriel began, "I've been meaning to talk to you about the band."

Oh no, thought Moshe Chaim, I can't talk about the band. I've got to think of a good excuse to get out of this conversation very quickly. Should I tell him that I have to go to the bathroom? Should I make believe my arm hurts?

Suddenly, Moshe Chaim's thoughts were interrupted.

Let's Do It Again!

Rabbi Goldsmith stuck his head in the classroom door.

"Gavriel," he said, "could you please go tell all the boys that recess is over?"

"Yes, right away," answered Gavriel.

Moshe Chaim breathed a sigh of relief. At least he wouldn't have to talk about the band.

After school, Gavriel tried to catch Moshe Chaim in front of the building, but by the time he got down the stairs, Moshe Chaim was already long gone.

"How does he disappear so fast with an injured knee?" Gavriel asked Binyamin.

"I don't know," answered Binyamin. "But right now, Yossi and I are going to Castle Park for our first baseball game of the season. I'm going to be pitching, and Yossi will be catching."

"That's great," said Gavriel. "Good luck. Shaya and I are going to go home and search the whole house for the song sheets. Don't forget to be on time for our practice this afternoon."

"We haven't missed one yet, have we, Yossi? We'll see you later."

Binyamin and Yossi headed for the Castle Park baseball field with all their friends.

Binyamin was really excited to walk up to the pitcher's mound. He had been waiting for this moment all winter long. How many times had he dreamed about throwing out the first pitch?

It was a great game.

Unbeknown to Binyamin, Moshe Chaim Kramer was standing among the trees in right field. Staying at home had been too lonely, and he had come to watch the game.

In the top of the ninth inning, with the score tied at one, Binyamin's teammate, Yaakov Weiner, hit a high fly ball to the outfield. It flew further and further and didn't stop until it landed in the cluster of trees at the end of the field.

"Home run!" yelled Binyamin and his teammates.

When their half of the inning was over, Binyamin and his teammates took the field.

"This is great," Binyamin called to his catcher Yossi. "All I have to do is keep the other team from scoring for one inning, and we win."

Unfortunately, things did not go as well as Binyamin had planned.

The first batter Binyamin faced was Shuey Waxman. Shuey swung hard at Binyamin's first pitch and hit a single. The next batter, Heshy Coleman, did the same.

Binyamin started to sweat very hard. He wasn't smiling any longer. The smile returned to his face, however, after he struck out the next two batters.

Binyamin was in control again and determined not to give up any more hits.

Unfortunately, this was not to be.

Binyamin was more surprised than anyone when Aryeh Blackman, the next batter, hit the very first pitch far into right field.

The right fielder scrambled to get the ball. He tried to throw out the runner at home plate, but it was too late. One boy had already scored, and the game was tied at two.

Let's Do It Again!

The next batter also reached base, and the bases were loaded.

As the next batter walked up to the plate, Binyamin's heart began to beat wildly.

If he let this batter get a hit, the other team would win. Binyamin knew that the next pitch he threw would be a very, very important one.

He looked toward his teammates in the field. Out of the corner of his eye, he saw Moshe Chaim standing among the trees watching the game.

What was he doing here?

This was not the time to worry about that. His whole team was counting on his next pitch.

Should he throw his famous underhand curve ball, or the old, reliable fastball?

This was a decision that was too hard to make on his own. Binyamin signaled a time out and called his catcher Yossi up to the mound.

"What pitch do you think I should throw next, Yossi?" Binyamin asked nervously.

"Hmm, that's a good question. Usually, your curveball is your best pitch, but that last batter really smacked it hard."

Yossi thought very hard about the matter.

"I would guess," he finally said, "that you should throw a fastball."

"That's a good idea," Binyamin agreed.

"Binyamin?" Yossi began.

"Yes," Binyamin answered.

"Well," continued Yossi, "something's been bothering me."

"What's the matter?" Binyamin asked nervously. "Am I throwing the ball the wrong way? Do I move my arm too far back before I throw a pitch?"

"No, no, no," Yossi answered. "It has nothing to do with your pitching. You've been throwing just great today."

"Then what's the problem?" Binyamin cried.

"I was just thinking about Moshe Chaim. He looks so sad standing there in right field. I wonder what he's thinking."

"What?" cried Binyamin. "It's the bottom of the ninth inning, the bases are loaded, and the score is tied, and all you can think about is what Moshe Chaim Kramer is thinking?"

"Yes," answered Yossi. "I'm a little worried about the way he's been acting. He looks so sad. I haven't heard him make one joke in the last few days."

"What's taking you guys so long?" came the cry from third base. "We've got a game to play, you know."

"We just need one more minute," Yossi called back. "Well, Binyamin, what do you think?"

"I think," said Binyamin, "that I can't believe you're asking me this question in the middle of a baseball game. Why don't we wait until later to discuss this, okay?"

"Okay," agreed Yossi. "We'll talk about it later. Right now, just throw a good fastball, and strike this next batter out."

As he prepared to throw the first pitch, Binyamin's mind played back his conversation with Yossi.

Hmm, he thought, as he drew back his arm. I am

a little worried about Moshe Chaim. He really has been acting strange lately. His sling and bandage really are mysterious, too. He doesn't seem to be limping at all in right field.

Binyamin released the ball.

The batter swung, just one second too late. Strike one.

The boys on Binyamin's team began to cheer him on.

"Come on, Binyamin," they cried from the field. "You can do it!"

Binyamin threw the next pitch for a second strike.

"Strike him out, Binyamin!" the boys yelled.

"Let's win this game!"

Binyamin, however, didn't hear a word they were saying. He was too busy thinking.

At such an important moment of his favorite sport, Binyamin Weintraub was amazed to find himself standing on the pitcher's mound but not thinking about baseball at all.

To his great surprise Binyamin could only think about one thing—his friend Moshe Chaim.

Why does he look so sad? he asked himself. There must be something really serious bothering Moshe Chaim to make him act like this.

He drew his arm back and then quickly propelled it forward, releasing the ball.

It glided gently through the air and sailed directly towards the center of Yossi's glove.

The batter steadied himself and swung with all his might. He missed. It was strike three, and the inning was over. The game was still tied.

It was finally Binyamin and Yossi's team's turn at bat again.

The first pitch thrown by the other team was blooped into the infield for a single.

The next batter hit a hard shot right over the head of the first baseman. There were men on first and second. Binyamin and all his teammates really started to get excited.

Yaakov Weiner then hit a hard line drive right to second base. The second baseman quickly stuck his glove out in front of him to catch the ball. Fortunately, he was a fraction of a second too late. Instead of landing in the glove, the ball bounced off the second baseman's thumb and landed in front of him. The bases were loaded.

The next batter hit a pop fly right to the left fielder for an easy out. The batter after him didn't do much better. He grounded out to third.

Once again, Binyamin's heart began to pound. After all his pitching, he really wanted to win this game.

The next batter hit a really hard line drive right between first and second base. The right fielder had been playing very deep and had to run in to make the play. He quickly grabbed for the ball and threw it to first base as fast as he could.

The runner was safe!

Or was he?

Binyamin's team sure seemed to think so. The other team, however, was just as sure that the runner was out.

Let's Do It Again!

An argument began.

"He was safe!"

"Are you blind or something? He was out!"

"Safe!"

"Out!"

"Boy," Binyamin whispered to Yossi. "This sounds like one of Gavriel and Dassie's fights."

"What are we going to do?" asked Yossi.

Binyamin smiled.

"I have a great idea," he said. "Maybe I can help cheer up Moshe Chaim, mystery and all."

Binyamin ran off toward right field.

"Moshe Chaim," he called, "can you come help us?"

Moshe Chaim had been sitting quietly under a tree, trying very hard to remain out of sight. Now his privacy was suddenly interrupted by Binyamin's cries.

"What's the matter, Binyamin?" he asked.

"Could you help us settle our argument?"

"How can he help?" asked Yaakov Weiner. "He probably wasn't even watching when the play was made."

"That's true," answered Moshe Chaim. "But I think I could help if I watched the play now."

"What do you mean?" asked Yossi.

"I mean," answered Moshe Chaim, "that I think you should show me exactly what happened, and I can tell you as an unbiased party if the runner was safe or out."

"That sounds like a good idea," agreed Binyamin.

"So, let's do it already," cried a boy from the other team.

All the players went back to the exact spots they

111

had been standing in when the play had been made. Then the runner made believe he was hitting the ball again. The right fielder once again threw the ball to first base and the first baseman caught it, at what everyone agreed to be the exact moment he had before.

"Aha," cried Moshe Chaim, with a smile. "I have the answer to the problem. Ahem." He cleared his throat loudly and began to state his ruling with a voice full of authority. "You see, the first baseman caught the ball at exactly the same time that the runner tagged the base. According to the rules, a tie on first base goes to the runner, and so, the runner is safe."

"Yeah," cried Shuey Waxman. "Moshe Chaim is right. The runner is safe. I guess you guys win."

"Yahoo!" cried Binyamin. "Thanks, Moshe Chaim."

In the bottom of the tenth inning, all three batters were retired in a row. The game was won! Unbelievable!

"That was a great game!" Yossi cried out, sticking out a hand towards Shuey.

"Yeah," agreed Shuey as he shook Yossi's hand. "It was one of the best games we ever had."

When Binyamin came home, he was very excited.

"Gavriel," he cried, when he saw his brother, "you should have seen the way I pitched today. I was great! We won the game."

"That's good," said Gavriel sadly. "I'm glad to see that at least one of us had a good day."

"What do you mean?" asked Binyamin.

"I mean," Gavriel answered, "that Shaya and I spent two hours looking all over the house, and we couldn't find those song sheets."

"Oh," said Binyamin.

"And also," continued Gavriel, "I've been trying to call Moshe Chaim all day, and he wasn't home."

"I know where he was," answered Binyamin.

"Where?" asked Gavriel.

"He was at the baseball field."

"At the baseball field?" cried Gavriel. "What was he doing there with all of those so-called injuries?"

"Well," answered Binyamin, "most of the time he was just sitting by himself behind the trees in the outfield, but then I helped cheer him up."

"You did?" asked Gavriel. "How did you do that?"

"It was simple," answered Binyamin. "I asked him to help us solve an argument between the two teams. You should have seen the look on his face when he solved our problem. It was the first time I saw him smile like that in a long time."

"Really?" said Gavriel thoughtfully.

He stopped, tilted his *yarmulka* to the front of his head and stroked an imaginary beard on his chin.

"Of course," he said. "Moshe Chaim loves to help people with their problems. That's why he smiled, and that's the way we can keep making him smile."

Gavriel turned toward his brother.

"Binyamin," he said, "you're a genius!"

"I am?" Binyamin asked.

"Yes," answered Gavriel. "You just told me how I'm going to get Moshe Chaim to tell me what's bothering him. I can't wait until tomorrow to find out. Thank you, Binyamin. You've really helped make my day."

CHAPTER SEVEN

Super Great

It was one very hard Monday morning for Gavriel Weintraub. He couldn't wait to speak to Moshe Chaim, but he had to sit through a whole morning of class first. He wanted very much to pay attention to what his *rebbi* was teaching, but it was so hard to stop thinking about the conversation he was planning to have with his friend.

Finally, it was time for recess. The entire class filed out of the room and began walking towards the backyard to play. Moshe Chaim Kramer, however, remained behind.

He was very surprised to see Gavriel Weintraub walk back into the room.

Gavriel smiled at his friend and walked over to his desk.

"Hi, Moshe Chaim," he said. "What's doing?"

"Nothing much," answered Moshe Chaim nervously.

"I've been meaning to talk to you, Moshe Chaim," said Gavriel. "I just never seem to have the chance."

Suddenly, their conversation was interrupted when Heshy Coleman burst into the room.

"Gavriel," he cried, all out of breath. "Come quickly!"

"What is it?" Gavriel asked. "Is something wrong?"

"You're not going to believe this, but Avi Gross just punched a ball past the oak tree in left field."

"I don't believe it!" cried Gavriel. "I was the only person who ever did that before."

"Well," said Heshy, "Avi just did it, too, and he thinks his ball went further than yours did. He wants you to come out and check."

"But I'm in the middle of speaking to Moshe Chaim now," Gavriel cried.

"You have to come now," Heshy yelled. "We want to finish the game already, and Avi won't let anyone touch the ball until you come and look at it."

"Oh, all right," Gavriel sighed. "I'm coming. I guess I'll have to speak to you later, Moshe Chaim."

Moshe Chaim breathed a sigh of relief. Once again, he had been saved from having to reveal his secret to anyone. He would have to run home very fast after school, before Gavriel would get a chance to try and speak to him again.

As soon as the class was dismissed, Moshe Chaim headed straight for the door. He walked as quickly as his fake limp would let him. He still had to make believe he was limping, because it was a good excuse to allow

115

him to stay by himself so that the boys wouldn't bother him too much about the band.

Once out of sight of all the boys from *yeshivah*, Moshe Chaim broke into a run. He wanted to get home as soon as possible. He did not want to meet up with Gavriel and all his questions.

Moshe Chaim was greatly relieved to turn the corner of the street where he lived. He ran faster than ever once his house was in sight.

Suddenly, Moshe Chaim stopped in his tracks and rubbed his eyes. He couldn't believe what he saw.

Standing, waiting patiently in front of the door to Moshe Chaim's house, was none other than Gavriel Weintraub.

"Wh . . . what are you doing here?" he stammered.

"Why, I'm waiting for you, Moshe Chaim," Gavriel answered.

Moshe Chaim swallowed hard. Had Gavriel seen him running? How could he not have? Uh oh. Then Gavriel knew that the bandage was a fake, and he probably knew that the sling was, too.

"Listen, Moshe Chaim," Gavriel began. "I need your help."

"You need my help?"

"Yes," said Gavriel. "I have a problem that I need you to help me solve."

"You do?"

"Yeah," said Gavriel. "You see, Shaya and I wrote up a bunch of song sheets with ideas for the band's new songs."

"So?" said Moshe Chaim.

"So," Gavriel continued, "I left them on my dining room table before I went to sleep *Motzei Shabbos*. When I woke up in the morning and went to get them before school, they were gone."

"Maybe somebody put them away somewhere," Moshe Chaim suggested.

"Well, the last person who saw them Sunday morning is my pain-in-the-neck little sister Dassie. She claims the papers were on the table that morning when she began to paint her pictures."

"So where did she put them?" asked Moshe Chaim.

"That's the funny thing," answered Gavriel. "She says she didn't do anything with them. But that can't be true. Shaya and I spent the whole afternoon looking for them yesterday, and we couldn't find them anywhere in my house."

"You think Dassie is lying?"

"Well," answered Gavriel, "I don't think I've ever heard her lie before, but she was the last person to see them, and we have been getting into a lot of fights lately."

"So you think she took them?"

"Maybe," said Gavriel. "I'm just not sure. That's my big problem, and I need some help solving it."

Gavriel turned to Moshe Chaim.

"Do you know what?" he said.

"What?" asked Moshe Chaim.

"Now that I've told you my problem, I don't feel so bad any more. Just talking about it made me feel better."

"Really?" asked Moshe Chaim.

"Really," answered Gavriel. "My mother always says that the best thing to do when you have a problem is to talk it over with someone, and that's what I just did. I'd be very happy to listen to you if you have any problems to tell over. Maybe I can make you feel better, too."

"Well," began Moshe Chaim, "I do sort of have a problem, and I also don't know how to solve it. The only problem is that I don't think anyone in the whole world can help me solve my problem."

"You never know what a friend can do," said Gavriel.

"Oh all right, I'll tell you already. I guess it's about time I did anyway.

"You see," Moshe Chaim continued, "I'm not in the Cheery Bim Band any more."

"What?" cried Gavriel.

"That's right," answered Moshe Chaim. "Do you remember last week when we had that surprise quiz?"

"Yes," answered Gavriel.

"Well," Moshe Chaim continued, "I did terribly on it. Or actually, I did fine on the first questions, but when it came to the last questions, on the stuff we learned in class since the band started, I really flubbed up. Rabbi Goldsmith spoke to my father and told him that I haven't been reviewing my work or paying attention in class."

"Uh oh," said Gavriel.

"That sure was an uh oh," agreed Moshe Chaim. "When my father discovered all the band posters I had made, he assumed I was thinking about the band too much and that it was interfering with my learning."

"Was he right?" Gavriel asked.

"I think so," answered Moshe Chaim. "So anyway, he told me that I am not allowed to have anything to do with the band."

"Is that why you've been missing practices and not showing up at Reb Velvel's store to clean?"

"Yes, and that's why I made up this great excuse with my wrist and knee to miss all that." Moshe Chaim raised the arm that was in the sling.

"I thought there was something strange about that sling, not to mention that ace bandage. No wonder you've been looking so depressed."

"Yes," sighed Moshe Chaim, "that's my problem, and I really don't think that there is anything anyone can do to help me solve it."

"Oh yes, there is," cried Gavriel.

"What?"

"Shaya and I can help you solve your problem," answered Gavriel.

"How?"

"Before I tell you how," answered Gavriel, "I'd like to make a little deal."

"What kind of deal?" asked Moshe Chaim.

"I'll help you with your problem," said Gavriel, "if you'll help me solve mine."

"That sounds like a good deal to me," said Moshe Chaim with a smile. "Now what's your plan?"

"Well," began Gavriel, "according to what you told me, the only reason your father isn't letting you be in the band is because you weren't learning well, so what would happen if you started learning well now?"

"I don't know," answered Moshe Chaim.

"What would happen if you were learning better than good? What would happen if you were learning super great?"

"I don't know," answered Moshe Chaim, "but how do you expect to accomplish all that in time for the *Hachnassas Sefer Torah?*"

"I think," said Gavriel, "that if you were learning super great, your father would agree to let you rejoin the band."

"Hmm," said Moshe Chaim, "do you really think so?"

"I'm sure of it," Gavriel answered with confidence.

"But how can I learn super great?" asked Moshe Chaim. "I've already missed so much, and there's so little time left."

"Aha!" cried Gavriel, "Shaya and I are going to help you learn super great."

"How?"

"This Thursday," continued Gavriel, "Rabbi Goldsmith is going to be giving us a big *Chumash* test, and you are going to get a hundred on it."

"I am?"

"You bet you are," cried Gavriel, "because from now until then, you, Shaya and me are going to spend every free minute we have, including recess, studying *Chumash*. We will learn together at night in Shaya's house, and when we get home, we can learn together over the phone."

"What?" cried Moshe Chaim. "You want to learn at

recess? I've never heard of anyone learning during recess."

"Well," said Gavriel, "there's always a first time for everything."

"Wait a minute!" cried Moshe Chaim. "Isn't Thursday the same day as the *Hachnassas Sefer Torah*?"

"That's right," answered Gavriel. "We are only having a half day of school that day. We'll ask Rebbi how you did, and then you can call your father and tell him. Then, I'm sure he'll let you come with us to play that afternoon."

"But when am I supposed to practice? I'll even miss the one you'll have Thursday morning."

"Hm, I didn't think about that," said Gavriel. "I guess you're right. You'll have to miss that practice."

"How can I miss all the practices before we play?"

"Don't worry," said Gavriel. "According to my calculations, we should have just enough time for one practice right after school. Besides, at least you were at the practices since *Lag Baomer* up until your, ahem, injury. We're playing the same stuff we practiced then. Don't worry, you'll do fine."

"But will one more practice be enough for me?" asked Moshe Chaim nervously.

"It's going to have to be enough," answered Gavriel. "Don't worry, Moshe Chaim, you're a good musician. You'll do okay. We'll let you know everything you need to be aware of when you come to the practice after school."

"If I ever come to it, you mean. I hope you're right. At any rate, I'll talk to my father about it, and if he agrees, I'll be at Shaya's house to learn tonight. Good-bye, Gavriel, and thanks."

"Good-bye, Moshe Chaim. See you later."

That night, when Gavriel went over to Shaya's house to learn, Moshe Chaim was there, too.

"What did your father say?" Gavriel asked Moshe Chaim before they sat down to learn.

"Well, you can't imagine how happy my father is that I'm here learning with you," he said. "He even volunteered to drive me here every night."

"So," Shaya asked, "does that mean he'll let you back in the band now?"

"What he told me is that when Rabbi Goldsmith called him a second time to tell him that I haven't been myself since the day he gave the quiz, he realized how important the band really was to me."

"Does that mean that even if your learning doesn't improve, he'll let you back in the band?" Shaya asked again.

"He feels that first I should realize that learning is still more important," Moshe Chaim replied.

"Okay, that's what we're here for," Gavriel responded. "He agreed to our deal then?"

"He said if I can get a top grade, he thinks I'll have learned how to balance things out."

"That's great," said Gavriel. "It means we have a chance."

"Yeah, I think he's just about as excited about this test as we are. He can't wait to see if this will work, and I'll pull through. I sure hope that all this will help."

"Don't worry," said Gavriel. "It will."

"So, what are we waiting for?" cried Shaya. "Let's start learning."

The boys quickly opened their *Chumashim.*

Soon they were transported back in time, to medieval France. They were sitting in the *beis medrash* of the great *tzaddik* Rashi, who explained to them the meaning of each and every *pasuk* with amazing clarity.

Not one second was spent thinking about the Cheery Bim Band. Tonight, in this house, all thoughts were of Torah.

As soon as Moshe Chaim's father came to pick him up, Gavriel ran to his own house. He was to learn with Moshe Chaim over the phone, and he wanted to be ready when his friend would call.

"What's going on here?" Miriam cried to her mother later that evening. "Gavriel has been on the phone for an hour already. If he keeps this up, I won't be able to speak to any of my friends tonight."

"Shh! Gavriel's learning."

"Over the phone?" Miriam asked.

"Why not?" Mrs. Weintraub answered. "To me it sounds as if Gavriel's learning better tonight than he ever did before. Look! He doesn't stop for a second."

"Okay," Miriam said. "I guess I can live without speaking to my friends for one night."

Suddenly, Dassie burst into the room, wearing her pink pajamas and banging a pot loudly with a spoon.

"CHIRRY BIM, CHIRRY BUM," she sang at the top of her lungs.

"Sh!" her big sister shushed her. "Gavriel's learning."

"So what?" asked Dassie. "Why can't I sing? It's not fair. Gavriel can sing whenever he wants, and I have to be quiet because he's on the phone."

Gavriel glared at his little sister angrily.

"Can't you keep quiet?" he cried.

"No, I can't!" answered Dassie angrily.

"Oh, great," cried Gavriel. "First, she takes away my song sheets, and now, she wants to take away my learning time, too."

"Gavriel," cried Miriam, "Dassie told you a thousand times that she didn't take those sheets of yours."

"Then where are they?" Gavriel asked.

"I don't know," answered Miriam, "but that doesn't mean Dassie took them."

"But she was the last one to see them!" Gavriel cried.

"That still doesn't mean that she took them."

"Then who did take them?"

"I don't know, Gavriel," Miriam answered. "Just stop picking on Dassie. She's only a little girl, you know."

"So what?"

"Gavriel, Miriam, Dassie," cried Mrs. Weintraub, "stop shouting this instant."

"It's their fault!" cried Gavriel.

"No, it's his," cried the girls.

"That's enough," said Mrs. Weintraub.

"Sisters, hmph, who needs them?"

"Brothers, hmph, who needs them?"

"Are you still on the phone, Moshe Chaim?" Gavriel asked.

"Yes, I am," answered Moshe Chaim. "Now could we get back to learning this Rashi?"

The next morning, Moshe Chaim walked into class looking much better than he had the day before. His bandage and sling were gone, and now a big smile rested on his freckled face. To Gavriel, he looked happier and more confident sitting at his desk today than he had all year.

"Good morning, boys!" Rabbi Goldsmith said as he walked in. "In order to help prepare for our big *Chumash* test, I am going to call on boys to read. The first piece which I will call upon someone to read is the Rashi on *pasuk gimmel* of *perek daled.*"

A few groans went up from the back of the room.

"Yes, boys," Rabbi Goldsmith said. "I know it is a very difficult piece to read, but we spent many days in class going over it. I, therefore, expect you all to know it."

The room grew silent.

"Now," Rabbi Goldsmith continued, "are there any boys who would like to volunteer to read for the class?"

That's the piece we learned last night, Gavriel thought to himself as he raised his hand.

Rabbi Goldsmith glanced around the room. Only a handful of boys had volunteered to read. The hands of Shaya Ginsberg, Asher Kaplan and Moishe Gelb, the three smartest boys in the class were, of course, the first ones raised.

Rabbi Goldsmith was pleased to see Gavriel Weintraub, Heshy Coleman and Zevy Grey raise their hands, too. What surprised him the most, however, was seeing Moshe Chaim Kramer's hand slowly rise.

Rabbi Goldsmith peered over the top of his glasses to make sure he was seeing properly.

It was not that Moshe Chaim had never raised his hand before, but after his poor performance in class the previous week, Moshe Chaim had been the last boy his *rebbi* would have expected to volunteer to read such a hard piece of Rashi. Most of the boys in class were simply afraid to do so.

"I said," he repeated once more just to make sure, "I would like a volunteer to read the Rashi of *pasuk gimmel* of *perek daled.*"

Moshe Chaim's hand remained hanging in the air.

"Moshe Chaim Kramer," Rabbi Goldsmith called, "would you like to read the Rashi?"

"Yes, I would."

"Please begin," Rabbi Goldsmith replied, eager to see what would happen.

Rabbi Goldsmith's mouth dropped wide open in shock as he heard Moshe Chaim's perfect reading and explanation of the words of the Rashi. He simply couldn't believe what he was hearing. Was this the same boy who hadn't known any answers just a few days before?

"That was excellent!" he cried happily when Moshe Chaim had finished. "I see you've been studying, Moshe Chaim. Keep it up."

Moshe Chaim smiled sheepishly, happy to hear the words of praise from his *rebbi*.

Soon the recess bell rang.

Let's Do It Again!

"Okay, boys, you can have your recess now," Rabbi Goldsmith announced.

"Gavriel! Moshe Chaim!" Avi Gross called. "We need you two to have fair teams for punchball. Can we choose you in?"

The two boys wanted nothing more than to go join in the game. Moshe Chaim turned to Gavriel.

"I'll leave it up to you," he said.

Gavriel's mind began to churn. Why shouldn't we play? he asked himself. We learned until very late last night, and we will again tonight, too. We're entitled to have a little fun. I don't think that missing twenty minutes of learning will hurt my test score at all. But what about Moshe Chaim? These twenty minutes might make a big difference to his grade on that test, and we really need him in the band.

"I'm sorry, Avi," Gavriel said. "We're not going to be able to play today."

"Are you sure?" Avi asked.

"I'm positive!"

Once again, Rabbi Goldsmith found himself in a state of shock. He couldn't believe what he was seeing.

Moshe Chaim, Shaya and Gavriel stayed behind in the class as the other boys rushed out to the yard.

"Aren't you boys going out to play?" he asked.

"If it's okay with you," Shaya replied, "we'd like to stay inside today and learn instead."

"It's not just okay," said Rabbi Goldsmith happily. "It's simply wonderful."

The three boys quickly gathered around Gavriel's desk, took out their *Chumashim* and began to learn.

Their *rebbi* looked on quietly with a proud smile on his lips.

"Where were you guys during recess?" Avi Gross asked Gavriel at the end of the day.

"We were in class learning, of course," Gavriel answered. "The *Chumash* test is only two days away, you know."

"Oh . . . yeah, of course," Avi answered thoughtfully.

Even Gavriel's family was amazed at the change in him.

"Are you going to learn while you're eating, too?" Binyamin asked Gavriel at the supper table that night.

"I just need to look at one more *pasuk* before I start to eat," Gavriel replied as he leafed through his *Chumash*.

"Boy," Binyamin said to Gavriel as they walked to school the next morning, "you and your *chavrusos* have really been learning up a storm. The whole school was talking about how you guys stayed in class to learn extra during recess yesterday."

"How did everyone find out about that?" Gavriel wondered out loud.

"Everyone knows about it," Binyamin laughed. "No one ever heard of boys staying in class to learn when they could be outside playing punchball. This has got to be the strangest thing to happen in our school in a long time."

"We're doing it again at recess today," Gavriel said.

"You guys are really amazing," said Binyamin. "I don't know if I'd be able to give up playing punchball for one day, and you guys are doing it for two."

"It's not that hard," Gavriel replied. "In fact, I really enjoy it."

During class, Moshe Chaim felt great. Rabbi Goldsmith called on him to answer three hard questions, and he got them all right.

He turned and smiled at Gavriel and Shaya. He couldn't wait until their recess study session.

Soon the recess bell rang.

"Okay, boys," Rabbi Goldsmith said. "You may go out to the yard for recess now."

Once again Gavriel, Shaya and Moshe Chaim were the only boys left in the room.

"Okay," said Shaya, opening his *Chumash*, "it's your turn to read, Gavriel."

Just as Gavriel was about to begin, the boys heard a noise coming from the classroom door.

Suddenly, to their great surprise, Avi Gross and Moishe Gelb walked back into the room. They sat down at their desks, took out their *Chumashim* and began to learn.

The three friends smiled at each other. It seemed as though other boys were beginning to learn from their example.

Suddenly, the classroom door opened once again. Zevy Grey and Asher Kaplan walked in, sat down at their desks and also began to learn.

"What's going on?" Moshe Chaim whispered.

"It would seem," said Shaya, "that other boys in the class have decided to follow our example and learn during recess."

To the boys' surprise, the classroom door did not stop opening. More and more boys continued to come in to learn.

A very pleasantly surprised Rabbi Goldsmith just sat behind his desk, grinning from ear to ear as he watched the classroom fill up with boys who wanted to learn.

Gavriel, Shaya and Moshe Chaim felt so good that they learned even better than they had the day before.

"Okay," said Moshe Chaim as the boys walked home from school, "Gavriel and Shaya, you've helped me with my problem, and now it's time for me to help with yours. Before I go home, I would like to go over to Gavriel's house and find those song sheets."

"Good," said Gavriel, "because we really must have them tonight. Tomorrow is the *Hachnassas Sefer Torah*, and tomorrow's two practices will be the only chance we'll have to practice our new song, if we ever find it."

"Oh yeah," groaned Yossi. "I forgot that we have to wake up early tomorrow. I hate doing that, but I know we really need every practice we can get."

"Easy for you to say," said Moshe Chaim. "At least you've been to all the practices. What's going to happen to me with just one practice left before we perform, if I'm even allowed to perform?"

"Don't worry, Moshe Chaim. You'll do just fine," Shaya said. "Just find us those song sheets, and everything will work out somehow."

"Just how are you planning to find the song sheets anyway?" Binyamin asked Moshe Chaim.

Let's Do It Again!

"Ahha!" cried Moshe Chaim. "I have a plan."

"What kind of plan?" asked Yossi.

"Well," began Moshe Chaim, "do you remember that baseball game the other day?"

"Of course," answered Binyamin. "How could we forget it? You really saved the day when you settled our argument."

"The same thing I did to settle their argument at the baseball game, I will do to settle Gavriel and Dassie's argument at home."

"What did you do?" asked Gavriel.

"I reenacted the play."

"You what?" asked Shaya.

"I made them make the play over again, showing me exactly what happened. That's what I'm going to do in Gavriel's house."

"Well," said Binyamin, as they approached his house, "we're here, so start reenacting."

"Wait a minute," said Moshe Chaim. "Before we go into the house, I want you to do me a favor."

"I'll do anything you want," said Gavriel, "as long as you find those papers."

"Good," said Moshe Chaim. "What I want you to do is go inside the house right now and apologize to your sister for getting into so many fights with her."

"What?" cried Gavriel. "She's the one who bothers me all the time, and you want me to apologize to her?"

"Yes," answered Moshe Chaim. "You're the big brother, and it's up to you to take the first step to make peace. Besides, I know you don't really like to fight with Dassie. This is your chance to make peace."

"Hm, maybe you're right, Moshe Chaim." Gavriel scratched his head. "Okay, I'll do it. I'll end the fight with Dassie right now."

Gavriel took a deep breath and quickly walked into the house and straight up the stairs to Dassie's bedroom.

"Uh oh," said Dassie when she saw her brother, "here comes another fight."

"No," said Gavriel, "you and I aren't going to fight any more, Dassie. I came up here to apologize for yelling at you, and I want to be friends again, okay?"

Dassie grinned from ear to ear. "Do you mean it, Gavriel?" she asked.

"Yes, I mean it," he answered.

"Oh goody!" she cried as she gave her brother a big hug. "I don't like fighting, and I don't want to do it any more."

Gavriel smiled. He really felt great.

"Now, Dassie," he began, "why don't you come downstairs with me? Moshe Chaim is here, and he says he's going to find those missing papers of mine. Maybe you can help."

"I didn't take them, Gavriel," Dassie said nervously.

"I believe you, Dassie," Gavriel answered with a smile. "Let's go."

Brother and sister went down the stairs together.

"Okay, Mr. Great Detective," Gavriel called to Moshe Chaim when he came downstairs, "let's see you find those missing papers."

"I will," said Moshe Chaim. "But I'm going to need everyone's help."

Let's Do It Again!

"What should we do?" asked Binyamin.

"Well," said Moshe Chaim, "I want you and Gavriel to go to bed."

"What?" cried Binyamin. "It's too early to go to sleep."

"I don't want you to go to sleep," answered Moshe Chaim, "I want you to go to your bedroom. Make believe it's Sunday morning again, and you're waking up and getting ready for school."

"Oh, I get it," said Shaya. "They're going to relive Sunday morning all over again to find where the song sheets went."

"Exactly!" answered Moshe Chaim. He turned to the little girl. "Now, Dassie, I want you to make believe it's Sunday morning again. I want you to get your watercolors and start painting at the table."

"How can it be Sunday and Wednesday?" asked the very confused little girl.

"Just pretend," Moshe Chaim said.

"Okay," said Dassie. "I'll go get my paints."

Dassie found her paint and paper, ran into the living room and sat down to paint.

"Is that just like you were doing on Sunday morning?" asked Moshe Chaim.

"No," answered Dassie with a giggle. "I can't even start to paint. I forgot to get my water. I guess it does feel like Sunday morning, though. I had to get up again then, too, for my water. But where's Gavriel's *Gemara*? He had it right there, you know, with some papers underneath it."

"I'll go get Gavriel's *Gemara*," Shaya volunteered.

"And I'll put a couple of blank sheets of paper under it instead of the song sheets."

"Now is everything the same as it was on Sunday morning?" Moshe Chaim asked when Shaya had put the *Gemara* in its place.

"No," said Dassie. "I have to get my cup of water, but that's just like it was Sunday, because I had to get up twice for the water then, too."

"Why?" asked Moshe Chaim, absently surveying the table.

"Because I spilled the first cup," Dassie replied.

Binyamin set down a cup of water beside Dassie.

"You see," Dassie continued, "I knocked the cup over just when I sat down to paint, and it spilled all over the table just like this."

Dassie purposely banged her elbow into the cup, knocking it over and spilling it all over the table.

"Hey!" cried Gavriel. "What are you doing? You're making a big mess, and it's getting all over my *Gemara*."

"I'm just doing what Moshe Chaim said," Dassie answered. "I'm doing everything just like I did on Sunday morning."

"Dassie's right," shouted Moshe Chaim. "Everything has to be exactly the way it was on Sunday."

"Okay, Gavriel and Binyamin," he continued, turning to the two brothers. "Go upstairs to your room, and come down the same way you did on Sunday."

The two boys ran up the stairs. When they reached the top they turned around and began walking down again.

Let's Do It Again!

Suddenly Binyamin stopped.

"What's the matter?" asked Gavriel. "Why are you stopping?"

"I stopped," Binyamin answered, "because we're not going down the stairs the same way we did on Sunday."

"What do you mean?"

"I mean that on Sunday we didn't walk down the stairs. We ran down."

"Oh yeah," cried Gavriel. "That's right. We were running, because we were late."

"So," said Moshe Chaim, "go back up to the top of the stairs, and come back down much faster."

Once again, the two boys climbed the stairs. This time, however, they ran as fast as they could on the way down. Gavriel ran into the dining room, rummaged under the wet pictures Dassie had already managed to paint for his *Gemara* and put it into his briefcase.

Suddenly, Moshe Chaim screamed.

"Aha!" he yelled. "We did it!"

"What did we do?" asked Gavriel.

"Why, we found the song sheets," answered Moshe Chaim.

"We did?"

"Of course we did," said Moshe Chaim. "Didn't you see what you just did?"

"All I did was put my *Gemara* into my briefcase," answered Gavriel.

"Yes," said Moshe Chaim, "but what about the pieces of paper that were underneath your *Gemara*?"

"Oh yeah," said Binyamin. "What happened to them?"

"I was watching very carefully," said Moshe Chaim, "and I noticed that when Gavriel picked up his *Gemara*, the wet papers stuck to the bottom of the *Gemara*. Gavriel put them in his briefcase without even realizing it."

"Oh!" cried Gavriel. "So that's what must have happened to the song sheets, too."

"That's right," said Moshe Chaim with a grin. "Those song sheets probably stuck to the bottom of your *Gemara* and then fell off in your briefcase when they dried."

"So," interrupted Shaya, "that would mean that the sheets should be somewhere in your briefcase."

The boys all ran towards the briefcase. Gavriel stuck in his hand and pulled out a whole pile of wrinkled papers.

Gavriel quickly sorted through them.

"Here they are!" he cried, holding up three sheets. "You did it, Moshe Chaim. Thanks a lot."

"Yahoo!"

"Hooray for Moshe Chaim!"

"*Yasher koach*, Moshe Chaim," said Gavriel giving his friend a hug. "You saved the day again."

"You're thanking me?" cried Moshe Chaim in dismay. "I'm the one who should be thanking you, Gavriel and Shaya. You're the ones who cured my silly fake injuries and gave me a chance to rejoin the band."

"That's what friends are for," answered Gavriel. He turned to Dassie. "Sorry, Dassie, for suspecting you."

Let's Do It Again!

"That's okay," the little girl replied with a giggle. "You just didn't know you took them yourself."

"Let's look through these song sheets quickly," Gavriel declared authoritatively, "and pick out our new song. It's getting really close to suppertime, and you guys have to go home."

The boys worked out the song, and Shaya, Moshe Chaim and Yossi headed home.

After supper, Gavriel went to Shaya's house to meet Shaya and Moshe Chaim for their learning *seder*. Binyamin decided to come along to listen in.

A few minutes after they got there, Moshe Chaim came in looking very excited.

"You'll never believe what happened, guys," he said.

"What now?" asked Binyamin.

"Well, when I said good-bye to you at Gavriel's house before, I thought I would go straight home to eat supper."

"So?" prodded Shaya anxiously. "We don't have all night, Moshe Chaim. We have a lot of learning to do."

"I didn't go straight home after all," said Moshe Chaim, ignoring Shaya's words, "because I suddenly remembered that I was supposed to pick up some bread and rolls for my mother from Katz's bakery. I headed towards Elm street, hoping that the bakery would still be open. When I got to the bakery the smell was unbelievably delicious. I felt like buying everything in the store."

"What does the smell in the bakery have to do with anything?" groaned Shaya.

"Like I said," Moshe Chaim continued, "the bakery smelled great, so I just stood there for a few minutes to enjoy the warm smell and look at all the delicious cakes. I especially liked the way the cupcakes with the sprinkles looked."

"Is this a very important part of the story?" Binyamin asked. "You're making me really hungry, Moshe Chaim."

"Yes," Moshe Chaim replied, "the cupcakes were very important, because as I was looking at them, I saw someone out of the corner of my eye."

"Who did you see?" asked Gavriel anxiously.

"I saw Rabbi Goldsmith," Moshe Chaim answered. "He was standing right in front of the bakery window, and you'll never believe to whom he was talking."

"Just tell us already, Moshe Chaim," Gavriel pleaded. "Don't make us guess."

"All right," continued Moshe Chaim, "Rabbi Gold- smith was standing outside the bakery talking to none other than my grandfather."

Moshe Chaim paused to take a breath.

"When I saw that," he continued, "I got really scared. The only thing that I could imagine them talking about was me. Who knew what Rebbi would have to say?

"I've been trying so hard to hide my poor learning from my grandfather. If Rabbi Goldsmith would give him a bad report about me, I would feel terrible. I would be so ashamed that I wouldn't be able to look at him again.

"I was so nervous, I could feel my heart beating faster than a racing car. Suddenly, my heart skipped a beat. I saw Rabbi Goldsmith and my grandfather begin to walk towards the bakery door. They were coming in!"

"What did you do?" asked Gavriel eagerly.

"I didn't know what to do," Moshe Chaim said. "I was terrified. I looked around and quickly ducked behind a display case, hoping they wouldn't see me. I had to stand there crouched behind the display for a whole ten minutes as Rebbi and my grandfather waited on line."

"That must have been terrible," said Shaya.

"You have no idea how terrible it was," Moshe Chaim sighed. "I had picked the display of cupcakes with sprinkles to hide behind, and boy was I hungry. I had to stand there for ten whole minutes with my mouth an inch away from those beautiful pink, red, orange and yellow sprinkles. That cake smelled unbelievably good. Standing there next to it was *mamish* torture!"

"Please!" Binyamin shouted, rubbing his stomach. "Stop talking about those cupcakes already."

"Finally," Moshe Chaim continued, "I saw Rabbi Goldsmith leave the store. I wanted to wait until my grandfather left, but I couldn't stand smelling those cupcakes any more. I just had to get out of there."

"So what did you do?" asked Gavriel.

"I waited until I was sure my grandfather was looking the other way, and I started to make a fast break for the door. I was sure he hadn't seen me. Suddenly, just as I was about to push open the door, I heard my grandfather call my name. I couldn't believe he had spotted me. Boy, did I think I was in big trouble."

"Can't you just get to the point already?" Shaya moaned.

"My grandfather," Moshe Chaim continued, "told me that he had just spoken to Rabbi Goldsmith and had gotten a full report about how I've been learning. I imagined how disappointed he must have felt in me, and I felt terrible. Suddenly, to my great surprise, my grandfather smiled. I couldn't believe what he said to me."

"What?" cried Gavriel anxiously. "Tell us already. What did he say?"

"He said that Rabbi Goldsmith told him that my learning was excellent!" Moshe Chaim laughed. "Can you believe that? I thought I was going to faint right there in the bakery."

Suddenly, Mrs. Ginsberg walked into the room.

"Hello, boys," she said. "I just finished baking and thought you all might like to come into the kitchen and have a little snack before you begin your learning."

"Mm." Binyamin rubbed his stomach. "I love everything you bake, Mrs. Ginsberg."

"Thank you very much, Binyamin. That's very nice of you to say."

"What did you bake, Mommy?" asked Shaya.

"Tonight," she answered, "I baked something which I haven't made in a long time. I made cupcakes with sprinkles."

"I'm really happy about what Rabbi Goldsmith

said," Gavriel said, as he took a bite out of his cupcake. "I also think that you've been learning really well, and if we really accomplish a lot of learning here tonight, I think you have a very good chance of getting a great mark on the test tomorrow, too."

"So, what are we waiting for?" cried Moshe Chaim, reaching for a *Chumash*. "Let's learn already."

CHAPTER EIGHT

Butterflies

Bzzzzzzzzzzzz.

Binyamin reached over to turn off the alarm clock.

"Gavriel," he called, "wake up. It's time for our early morning practice."

He heard no response.

"Come on, Gavriel," Binyamin yelled at the pile of blankets. "We can't be late. We have so little time left to practice. Please wake up now."

Suddenly, the bedroom door opened.

"Good morning, Binyamin," a cheery voice cried from the other side of the door.

"Gavriel?" Binyamin yelled. "What are you doing up? I thought you were still in bed. Wow! You're dressed already."

"Of course," replied Gavriel. "I've been up for half an hour."

Let's Do It Again!

Binyamin stopped and slapped his forehead.

"I forgot!" he cried. "Today's the big day you've been preparing for. The day of the big *Chumash* test."

"That's why I woke up so early," Gavriel said. "I was so nervous about the test that I could barely sleep. Whenever I did manage to doze off, I kept having this nightmare over and over again. I kept dreaming that I was sitting in class, and my *rebbi* handed me a test paper. I looked at it and didn't know the answer to one single question. My heart started pounding, and I broke out in a cold sweat."

"Then what happened?" asked Binyamin eagerly.

"I woke up," Gavriel answered. "*Oy*, I'm so worried about that test."

"Why in the world should you have anything to worry about?" asked Binyamin. "You've been studying for just about every single second during the last three days. You even studied during recess."

"I'm not so worried about me," said Gavriel. "I'm more worried about Moshe Chaim. If he doesn't do well, he can't play with our band any more. We're going to look pretty silly if we don't have Moshe Chaim there playing the drums."

"I'm sure he'll do okay on the test."

"I hope you're right."

"Look," Binyamin cried, glancing out the window. "There's Shaya across the street."

"Hey, Shaya," he called, leaning out the open window. "Wait for us."

Shaya did not answer.

"What's the matter with him?" Binyamin asked.

"How come he didn't hear me?"

"What did you say?" asked Gavriel.

"Oh no, not you, too?" cried Binyamin.

"I was just thinking about that Rashi we learned last night. I hope Moshe Chaim understood it well enough."

"I guess Shaya was, too," Binyamin said. "That must be why he didn't hear me."

"Come on, let's go," Gavriel called to his brother.

"Uh oh!" Gavriel cried when they had almost reached Reb Velvel's store.

"Did you just say uh oh?" asked Binyamin.

"I just remembered something I forgot to do."

"What did you forget?" Binyamin asked.

"I forgot to tell Reb Velvel that we were coming to have an early practice."

"What did you say?" asked Shaya, walking towards them.

"Gavriel forgot to tell Reb Velvel that we were coming for an early morning practice."

"You mean we dragged ourselves out of bed this early in the morning for nothing?"

Yossi suddenly came jogging up the block.

"What's going on, guys?" he asked. "How come no one's going inside?"

"Gavriel forgot to tell Reb Velvel that we were coming."

"You're kidding," Yossi cried. "Maybe we can go home and sleep for an hour before school starts."

"Wait a minute!" cried Gavriel. "We didn't even look into the store. Maybe Reb Velvel is up already anyway."

Let's Do It Again!

"Why would he be up this early if we didn't tell him we were coming?"

"Some people like to wake up early every morning," said Shaya.

"Why would anyone want to wake up early every morning?" asked Yossi with a yawn.

"Let's just look inside," said Gavriel.

"Hey," cried Shaya, "who's singing?"

All heads turned to see the source of the singing.

"I don't believe it!" said Shaya. "It's Reb Velvel! What's he doing out on the street so early in the morning?"

The boys all stood and watched in amazement as the old man walked briskly towards them. A merry chirry bim tune flowed from his lips.

"Good morning, Cheery Bim Band," Reb Velvel cried. "It is good to see you on this very fine day."

"Good morning, Reb Velvel," all the boys said together.

"I assume you have come to practice for the *Hachnassas Sefer Torah*," he said.

"You knew we were coming?" asked Binyamin in wonder.

"Of course," said Reb Velvel. "I know that you boys understand the importance of every moment. Today's the big day. I knew you would want to make the most of it."

"Where were you coming from at such an early hour of the morning?" asked Gavriel.

"Why I was coming from *shul* of course. I always try to *daven* at the earliest *minyan* that I can."

The Cheery Bim Band

"You mean you like to wake up this early?" Binyamin asked.

"Each morning," said Reb Velvel, "I like to wake up as early as I can, so I can go to *shul* and thank my Creator as soon as possible."

"I'd never be able to wake up so early every day," said Gavriel.

"By the way, boys," said Reb Velvel, "you don't have to worry about disturbing my neighbors. I already spoke to them, and they all agreed that it is perfectly fine with them if you want to practice at this early hour. It seems that they really enjoy listening to your wonderful music at any hour."

The boys quickly headed to the back of the shop.

"Let's get going already," said Shaya. "It's almost six-thirty. We only have one hour to practice."

Gavriel lovingly ran his hands along the keys of his keyboard.

Shaya caressed his clarinet.

Yossi gave his accordion a tight squeeze.

Binyamin blew a soft gentle blow into his recorder.

The boys looked at each other and smiled sadly.

Although they were quite happy to be playing their music together on the day of the *Hachnassas Sefer Torah*, they couldn't help but stare sadly at the empty seat in front of Moshe Chaim's drum set. Would he be there to join them this afternoon?

"Let's practice *Simen Tov* first," Gavriel suggested. "That's probably what everyone will sing when the new *Sefer Torah* is brought in."

Everyone nodded in agreement.

Let's Do It Again!

"Okay," said Gavriel. "Let's start from the beginning, the way we always sing it."

"One . . . and a two . . . and a three . . . *Simen tov umazel tov yehay lanu . . .*"

These happy words didn't seem as joyous as they usually did. A good friend and major part of the band was missing.

"*Simen tov umazel tov yehay lanu ulechal Yisrael . . .*"

Gavriel's hands looked like two blurs, as they flew up and down the long line of shiny black and white keys.

"*Simen tov umazel tov yehay lanu . . .*"

Shaya stood with his precious black clarinet suspended in front of him. Though he was happy that the band was playing together, it was just too bad that Moshe Chaim could not be here with them.

"*Ulechal Yisrael amen . . .*"

Reb Velvel stuck his head into the room and smiled at the boys. He took one step inside, lifted his arms up in the air and began doing a little dance.

"*Simen tov umazel tov yehay lanu . . .*"

He danced with the energy of a man fifty years younger than him, but the boys didn't even seem to notice.

"*Simen tov umazel tov yehay lanu ulechal Yisrael . . .*"

Reb Velvel looked around at the sad faces before him.

"*Simen tov umazel tov yehay lanu . . .*"

"Hold it, boys!" he yelled, over the din of the music.

The Cheery Bim Band

"Please stop playing!"

"What's the matter, Reb Velvel?" asked Gavriel as his hands dropped down from his keyboard. "Are we playing the song off key or something?"

"Yes," the old man answered. "You are playing this song terribly."

"We are?" asked Shaya nervously.

"You most certainly are," replied Reb Velvel.

"You see," he continued, "the purpose of your beautiful music is to make everyone happy. Only happy music can do that, and you are playing sad music."

"We are?" asked Binyamin. "But I always thought that *Simen Tov* was a happy song."

"You are right, Binyamin," replied Reb Velvel. "*Simen Tov* is supposed to be a happy song, but one cannot make happy music if one is sad."

"Oh," said Gavriel. "You can tell we're all sad?"

"Of course," said Reb Velvel. "You are sad, so your music is sad. Such wonderful boys like you should always be happy. What is bothering you so much today?"

"Well," said Gavriel, "Moshe Chaim's father said that he can't play with the band any more."

"*Oy!*" moaned Reb Velvel. "This is terrible. Mr. Kramer is such a nice man. Why would he say such a thing?"

"Because," answered Binyamin, "he thought Moshe Chaim was spending more time working for the band than he was with his learning."

"But don't worry," said Gavriel. "We've been doing

148

a lot of learning with Moshe Chaim this week, and he really knows his stuff. We're hoping that he gets a good mark on his *Chumash* test today. If he does, his father said he will let him back into the band."

"Ah," cried Reb Velvel, "such wonderful boys. They're worth a million dollars each. They help their friend so much when he needs them. They care for him so much. Ah, the members of this band are *mamish* diamonds."

"But what should we do about our music?" asked Shaya.

"Don't you worry, boys," he answered. "You just go to *yeshivah* and take that *Chumash* test. I'm sure everything will work out wonderfully for a bunch of boys who care so much for one another."

"I hope you're right," said Gavriel.

"Don't worry," said Reb Velvel with a wink. "Everything will work out just fine."

"Okay," said the boys, putting away their instruments. "Good-bye, Reb Velvel."

"Good-bye, boys," he answered. "Learn well in *yeshivah*, and don't worry."

"I can't stand it," Moshe Chaim said to his friends when he met them in *yeshivah*. "I'm so nervous that I can't do anything. My hands are shaking so much that it took me ten minutes just to put on my socks this morning. I had to retie my shoes four times until I got the bow right. My stomach feels like chopped liver."

"I know what you mean," said Gavriel, holding his own stomach. "It feels like I have twenty butterflies in there trying to get out."

The Cheery Bim Band

"You've got those butterflies, too?" Moshe Chaim chuckled. "Maybe I caught them from you."

During *davening*, Gavriel prayed with more *kavanah* than he had in a long time. He didn't look out of his *siddur* once the whole time. He just kept on *davening*, trying very hard to understand the meaning of each word his lips said.

While *davening*, Gavriel kept the *Chumash* test in mind. In his *tefillos*, he asked that Reb Velvel be right and that Moshe Chaim should indeed do well on the test he was about to take. The band really needed him.

After a recess spent with last minute cramming, it was time for the *Chumash* test. The boys all wished each other luck as they walked over to their seats.

As he sat down at his desk, Gavriel felt even more nervous than before.

It really feels like there are little butterflies fluttering around inside my stomach, he thought to himself.

When Rabbi Goldsmith entered the room, the heart of every boy began to beat a little faster.

"Well, boys." He smiled. "This is it. The moment we've all been waiting for so anxiously." He raised a stack of papers. "In my hand I hold the one and only *Chumash* test."

Gavriel swallowed hard. Boy, was he scared. He was always a little nervous before a test, but today he had two people to be nervous for, himself and Moshe Chaim.

"Before I give you your test," Rabbi Goldsmith continued, "I want to let you boys know that, no matter what grades you all get, I will always be very proud of you. You are a very fine group of boys, and your learning this year has been excellent."

Shaya took off his glasses and began rubbing his eyes. He was usually a very good test taker. Today, however, besides being nervous about his own test, he was worried about Moshe Chaim, too. Moshe Chaim was a good friend and a very important member of the band, and Shaya really wanted to see him do well.

Rabbi Goldsmith walked around the room, leaving a pile of papers face down on each boy's desk.

Seeing the actual test lying on his desk made Moshe Chaim's heart thump loudly. He wondered if the boys sitting next to him could hear it. His stomach felt like it did when he had gone on that roller coaster on *Chol Hamoed Sukkos*.

"You may now begin," he heard his *rebbi* say. "Good luck, boys."

Gavriel quickly ruffled through the pages of the test on his desk.

Seven pages? he thought to himself. It'll take me two hours to answer so many questions. I guess I don't have any other choice than to get started.

Hey, wait a minute, he thought, as he looked over the first few questions. These are easy. Maybe this isn't such a hard test after all.

He felt the nervous butterflies leave his stomach.

Gavriel turned to look at Moshe Chaim.

I hope Moshe Chaim remembers everything we learned, he thought to himself. He's worked so hard these past few days. He really deserves to get a good mark.

The Cheery Bim Band

The butterflies returned.

If Moshe Chaim fails, Gavriel thought to himself, he definitely won't be able to rejoin the band. Come on, Moshe Chaim. Get those answers right.

He turned to look at his friend.

Moshe Chaim sat perfectly still, staring at the pile of white papers in front of him.

What am I going to do? Moshe Chaim asked himself over and over again. I can't take this test. I'll flunk for sure. Then I'll get left back, and I'll have to be in seventh grade again next year. My stomach feels like it did when I ate that banana and peanut butter pizza at my cousin Shmulie's house last year. Maybe I'm sick! If I'm sick, I could tell Rebbi, and he'll send me home. Then I won't have to take this test. If I don't take it, I can't flunk. Nah, I can't do that. After all the work I put in studying, I can't miss this test.

Hey, wait a second, I put in a lot of time studying for this test. I should know something. Or did I forget everything?

That's it! I probably forgot everything I learned with Gavriel and Shaya. I probably won't know the answer to one single question. *Oy*, what am I going to do?

Wait a minute, he thought. What am I so nervous about? I've been studying for this test for the past three whole days. I knew all the answers to Rebbi's questions in class yesterday, so why shouldn't I know the answers to these questions on the test?

Moshe Chaim took a deep breath and picked up the pile of papers. He flipped them over to the front and looked at the first question.

Let's Do It Again!

He felt like doing a somersault and screaming in joy.

Hey! I know this one, I learned that with Gavriel on the phone last night.

Oh wow! Number two is even easier. It's the same question Rebbi asked me in class yesterday.

A huge smile spread across Moshe Chaim's face, as he felt those butterflies fly out of his stomach.

Maybe I won't do so badly after all, he thought.

SCRATCH SCRATCH SCRATCH . . . TICK TICK TICK . . .

The only noise which could be heard in the classroom was the soft sound of pens, scratching paper and the ticking of the clock.

TICK TICK . . .

Gavriel looked up at the clock. He had never realized it made such a loud noise before. Actually, he had never realized that it made any noise at all. The sound of his *rebbi's* voice usually drowned out the ticking noise. Today, however, Rabbi Goldsmith sat quietly at his desk, learning from a *sefer*.

Slowly but surely the boys worked their way through the long list of questions. It wasn't an easy test. The boys' minds had to jump constantly back and forth between the different *perakim* and *pesukim* they had learned.

It was a very fair test, though. The answer to every question had been thoroughly taught and reviewed by Rabbi Goldsmith many times.

With a big smile on his face, Moshe Chaim went through the first page of questions very quickly. He was pleasantly surprised at how much he actually knew.

Suddenly, he came to a question that made the smile on his face disappear.

Oh no! he moaned, I don't know the answer to this question. It must be from that last *pasuk* of *perek yud-alef*, which we didn't have enough time to learn over.

That's it, I'm doomed!

I bet all the rest of the questions are from that *pasuk*, too. I'll get them all wrong, then I'll fail the test and get left back.

Maybe being left back a grade won't be so bad, he tried to console himself. After all, Binyamin and Yossi will be in my class. I'll have to skip this question.

He turned to the next page of the test.

All right! he felt like screaming. A question from *perek gimmel*. I know the answer to this one and the next one, too.

Across the room, Gavriel was studying Moshe Chaim's face.

Hey, Gavriel thought to himself, Moshe Chaim still has a smile on his face. I guess he's doing okay, after all.

TICK TICK . . .

Oh no! Moshe Chaim wanted to scream as he looked at the clock. There are only five minutes left to the test, and I have one whole page more to go.

I'm doomed! he thought to himself as he glanced at the last page. There are twelve questions on this page. It's impossible for me to answer twelve questions in five minutes. I won't be able to do more than the first three questions. I'll have to leave the last nine questions blank.

Moshe Chaim swallowed hard.

Now I know I'll fail this test for sure. I've already skipped a few hard questions. How can I possibly pass if I skip nine more?

Moshe Chaim's heart beat loudly, and sweat dripped down his forehead. I'm in big, big trouble now. What do I do? What do I do?

Maybe I should say some *Tehillim*, he thought to himself. Yeah, that's it, Rebbi always told us stories about people who said *Tehillim* when they were in trouble, and everything worked out okay. *Oy*, but how could things possibly be okay? It's impossible for me to answer so many questions in such a short time. I might as well try the *Tehillim*, I've got nothing to lose.

"Oh, excuse me, boys," came Rabbi Goldsmith's voice from the front of the room. "I just wanted to remind you to follow the instructions written on the last page of the test."

"What instructions?" asked Avi Gross. "You mean this little box on top of the page?"

"Yes," Rabbi Goldsmith answered. "Please read the words written in that little box very carefully, boys."

What box? Moshe Chaim thought to himself, as he scanned the paper. I don't see any box!

Suddenly, his eyes fell upon a small black box drawn at the top of the page. In it was written two very short sentences.

"You may choose to answer any three of the twelve questions on this page. Good luck!"

I only have to answer three questions?

Yahoo! Moshe Chaim screamed in his mind. That's great! I don't believe it. I hardly even started to say *Tehillim*, and already everything worked out. Moshe Chaim picked up his pen and began to write the answers to the three questions he thought he knew best.

Just as he had finished writing the last answer, Rabbi Goldsmith's voice was again heard from the front of the room.

"Okay, boys," he said. "Your time is now up. Please put down your pens, and I will come around to collect your papers."

Rabbi Goldsmith quickly walked around the room, collecting the papers. The boys all leapt out of their seats and began to mill around the room. Gavriel and Shaya surrounded Moshe Chaim's desk.

"Well?" they asked eagerly. "How was it?"

Moshe Chaim didn't answer. He just sat still, his lips moving back and forth quietly reciting words of *Tehillim*.

"What are you doing?" Gavriel asked.

"I think he's *bentching*," said Shaya.

"Why are you *bentching* now?" asked Gavriel. "You didn't eat any bread."

"I wasn't *bentching*," replied Moshe Chaim with a smile. "I was just finishing something that I started during the test."

"Huh?"

"Never mind," said Moshe Chaim. "What did you guys think of the test? I thought it was pretty easy."

Let's Do It Again!

"You did?" cried Shaya.

"Yippee!" Gavriel shouted.

"Don't get so excited," said Moshe Chaim. "I said that I thought it was easy, but it could be that I got some questions wrong."

"So what's wrong with getting a few questions wrong?" asked Shaya.

"The problem is," answered Moshe Chaim, "that according to the deal I made with my father, the only way that I can rejoin the band is if I get a very good mark."

"Oh yeah," said Shaya nervously, "I forgot about that."

The three boys looked up towards the front of the room in time to see their *rebbi* put the test papers inside his briefcase and close it with a snap. He then put his hat on his head and donned his jacket.

"*Nu*, boys, what are you waiting for?" he declared to the class full of boys. "Why don't you all go home and get ready for the *Hachnassas Sefer Torah*?"

A roar of delight rippled through the classroom as all the boys pushed back their chairs and headed towards the door. All the boys, that is, except the three members of the Cheery Bim Band. They remained standing next to Moshe Chaim's desk as if stunned.

"What now?" Shaya asked, turning towards Gavriel.

"I don't know, but we better think of something fast," was Gavriel's reply.

"I see Rabbi Goldsmith out in the parking lot," Moshe Chaim cried out, pointing towards the window.

Without another word, the boys ran out the door

157

towards the parking lot, just in time to see Rabbi Goldsmith pull out.

"Come on, guys! We've got to stop him," called out Moshe Chaim as he vaulted the fence between the parking lot and the street.

Gavriel followed in hot pursuit. Shaya paused at the fence, looked at his two friends frantically waving their arms trying to flag down Rebbi as he passed. He clambered over to join them and was just in time to see Rabbi Goldsmith screech to a stop.

"What's this all about?" he asked, leaning out the car window.

"Well you see," Gavriel began, trying to catch his breath.

"It's like this," Moshe Chaim took over. "We didn't . . ." pant, pant "think . . ." pant "that you wouldn't be grading the tests."

"Moshe Chaim needs to know his test results for his father," Shaya explained, seeing Rabbi Goldsmith's confused look. "We were hoping that maybe you could spare a few minutes now to grade Moshe Chaim's test and let him know the results. His father is willing to let him rejoin the band in time to play for the *Hachnassas Sefer Torah* if he's done well enough."

Rabbi Goldsmith got out of the car, briefcase in hand. "You three were willing to give up all of your recess time these past few days towards preparing for this test. It's certainly the least I can do to give up a little of my free time to grade Moshe Chaim's paper."

He opened his briefcase and shuffled through the stack of papers until he came to Moshe Chaim's test paper. He pulled out his red pen and began reading the test.

Moshe Chaim felt his heart beating louder than a bongo drum. His hands were shaking, and his head was dripping with sweat. Maybe he hadn't done so well on the test. Maybe he had even flunked it. He couldn't bear to stand there watching Rebbi's every move. He turned around and began to pace from the curb to the *yeshivah* parking lot and back to the curb.

Gavriel and Shaya went over to a tree and sat down in its shade to await the outcome.

Finally, after what seemed like an eternity, Rabbi Goldsmith motioned Moshe Chaim over. After a short consultation, Rabbi Goldsmith climbed into his car and drove off.

"*Nu?*" cried Shaya anxiously, as he and Gavriel came running over. "What happened?"

"Well," said Moshe Chaim sadly. "I didn't exactly get the grade I was expecting."

"What?" cried Gavriel. "Oh no! Don't tell me you flunked the test."

"Now he won't be able to be in the band," moaned Shaya. "What are we going to do?"

"What grade did you get on the test?" asked Gavriel.

"Well," stammered Moshe Chaim, "like I said, I didn't get anything near the grade I expected to. You see, I expected to get about a seventy or eighty, and I got a *ninety-eight!* Ha ha! Can you believe it, guys? I got a *ninety-eight on the test!*"

"Yahoo!" cried Gavriel. "The Cheery Bim Band pulls through once again!"

"Yippee!" shouted Shaya. "You really had us worried there for a second."

"I can't believe it," Moshe Chaim cried. "Rabbi Goldsmith said he was very proud of the *hasmadah* we showed in our learning. He said he was very pleased with the example we set by learning during recess."

"I'm very happy," said Gavriel, "but right now we've got to get to Reb Velvel's store to practice."

"Wait a minute!" cried Moshe Chaim. "I can't go with you to practice just yet. My father is probably waiting near the phone to hear how I did."

"Oh yeah," responded Gavriel. "Give him a call now, and let him know the good news."

The boys ran down the block to the phone booth. Moshe Chaim searched his pockets and pulled out a quarter, which he plunked into the phone.

"Hello," he said.

"Yes, yes, so how did it go, Moshe Chaim?" his father asked eagerly.

"Well," began Moshe Chaim, "first of all I thought I should tell you that I've been doing a lot of thinking about what you said about how I was doing more band work than learning. I think you've seen how well my learning has been the past week."

"It certainly appears like you've improved, son," Mr Kramer's voice came over the phone. "But you know that the proof we both needed was this *Chumash* test. So tell me already. How did it go?"

"Well," Moshe Chaim declared happily, "I just got a ninety-eight on my *Chumash* test!"

"A *ninety-eight*?" his father shouted into the phone.

Let's Do It Again!

"That's really great, Moshe Chaim. Congratulations! That's even better than I expected. Provided you keep it up of course, you can certainly count yourself back in the band."

"Thanks so much," Moshe Chaim sighed happily into the phone. "And don't worry. I'm going to try not to let anything else get in the way of my learning ever again."

"Good luck."

Moshe Chaim hung up the phone. "So what are we waiting for?" he cried. "Let's get moving!"

"All right!" said Gavriel. "The Cheery Bim Band is back in business!"

CHAPTER NINE

The Old Clunker

The members of the Cheery Bim Band raced through the streets of Riverport towards Reb Velvel's store. There was not much time to practice, and they were very eager to begin.

It was not very long before the boys once again found themselves standing in front of the old second-hand music shop.

"Welcome back, boys!" Reb Velvel said as they walked in.

"Hello, Reb Velvel," they all shouted.

"Guess what!" Moshe Chaim said proudly. "I got a ninety-eight on my *Chumash* test today."

"That's wonderful!" Reb Velvel said. "Simply wonderful. I always knew that you would all develop into fine *talmidei chachamim*, and now I see that you're already on your way."

Let's Do It Again!

"And now I'm back in the band again!" Moshe Chaim shouted with joy.

"Yes, yes," said Reb Velvel. "This is good news indeed. You are a very special boy, Moshe Chaim, and a very important part of your band. It is certainly good to hear that you are back again."

"Please excuse us, Reb Velvel," Gavriel said politely, "but we have to start practicing as soon as we can."

"Of course!" cried Reb Velvel. "Practice makes perfect you know. A person can never practice anything too much. Hurry, go to your room and begin playing your beautiful music."

"Let's go, guys," Gavriel said, and they all ran to the back of the store.

The boys picked up their instruments. Gavriel gave the signal, and once again, Riverport's only second-hand music shop was filled with the sound of music. One song after another flowed out of the room in back of the store.

Reb Velvel sat in the front of the store behind the counter singing along with the music.

"Some stores play a stereo," he proudly told one customer, "but this store has a live band."

The customer smiled in reply.

"Remember, boys," Reb Velvel shouted towards the back of the store, "play with *simchah*, with happiness. When you feel happy, your music will sound happy. When your music sounds happy, everyone who hears it will be happy, too. Try to imagine that the musical notes you are playing are dancing around that new *Sefer Torah*."

The Cheery Bim Band

After the boys had played all the songs they had selected, they began to practice their new song. Over and over, they sang the words until they were sure they knew every last word and every last note by heart.

Finally, Gavriel glanced at his watch and realized that it was time to go.

"Okay, guys," he said. "We're going to have to start playing in a little under an hour, so we'd better start moving."

"Before we do anything," Shaya said, "I have one question to ask."

"What's the question?" asked Gavriel.

"What I would like to know," replied Shaya, "is how in the world are we going to get our equipment over to Beis Knesses Hagadol? It's all the way on the other side of town."

"Oh no!" Gavriel cried. "I forgot about that."

"We're really in trouble now!" said Moshe Chaim.

"We'll have to try to get a ride to the *shul*," Yossi declared.

"That's true," said Gavriel. "Let's try our parents and ask them if they could drive us."

"We'd better ask Reb Velvel if we can use his phone."

The boys quickly ran to the front of the store.

"Of course you may use my phone!" said Reb Velvel. "You boys are welcome to make as many phone calls as you like whenever you are here."

"I'll try my house first," said Gavriel. "Maybe my mother can drive us."

He picked up the phone and dialed the number.

Let's Do It Again!

"Nope!" he cried. "Nobody answers at my house. Why don't you try calling your house, Shaya?"

Shaya dialed his phone number. He spoke for a moment, then he sadly shook his head as he hung up the receiver.

"I'm sorry, fellas," he said, "but my father's car broke down, and my parents are getting a ride to the *Hachnassas Sefer Torah* in my neighbor's car."

"Why don't you try your house, Moshe Chaim?" he suggested. "Maybe you'll have better luck."

"I doubt I'll have any luck at all," Moshe Chaim replied. "My father is supposed to be going straight to the *shul* from work. My mother is going with my aunt."

All eyes turned toward Yossi Belsky.

"I guess it's up to you, Yossi," Gavriel said, handing him the phone.

"I'll call my father at his *sefarim* store," said Yossi.

He took the phone from Gavriel and quickly dialed the number.

"Hello," he said into the phone. "I'm here in Reb Velvel's store with the band, and we just realized that we don't have any way of getting to the *Hachnassas Sefer Torah*. Do you think you could give us a ride to the *shul*? . . . What? . . . Are you sure he won't be back in time? . . . Okay, I guess we'll have to find another way to go."

"What happened?" asked Gavriel eagerly.

"Well," Yossi reported sadly, "my father told me that he gave his assistant his car to make some deliveries. My father said that he's walking to the *Hachnassas Sefer Torah* after he closes the store later."

165

The Cheery Bim Band

"This is ridiculous!" Gavriel cried. "How are we ever going to get to the *Hachnassas Sefer Torah* without a car? Mr. Kramer wants us to start playing at five o'clock, and now it's already after four."

"I guess we're just going to have to carry all this stuff ourselves somehow," Shaya sighed.

"Oh no!" cried Moshe Chaim. "I'm not shlepping my whole set of drums all the way to the other end of town. I could, *chas veshalom*, get a hernia."

"Do you have any better ideas?" Gavriel asked him.

"I think I do!" said Reb Velvel.

"You?" asked the boys.

"I believe," said Reb Velvel, "that I may be able to get you boys a ride to the *shul*."

"You can?"

"Yes," he said, "I know someone who lives nearby that has a car. I'm sure that he would be honored to drive you."

"Who is it that's going to drive us?" asked Gavriel.

"Me!" answered Reb Velvel.

"You?" asked Gavriel.

"I didn't know you had a car!" said Shaya.

"Oh yes," said Reb Velvel. "I have a very wonderful car. I just don't drive it very often."

"Where is this car?" Moshe Chaim asked.

"It's right down the block," answered Reb Velvel. "One of my neighbors is nice enough to let me leave it parked in his garage."

"That's great!" said Gavriel. "Do you think you could drive us right now?"

"It would be my pleasure! I was going to close early

anyway for the *Hachnassas Sefer Torah*," Reb Velvel
responded. "Why don't you boys go to your back room
and bring out your equipment while I get the car."

"All right!" Moshe Chaim said as they made their
way to the back room. "I can't imagine how we would
have been able to carry all this stuff without Reb
Velvel's help."

Binyamin helped Moshe Chaim with his drums,
and Shaya helped Gavriel carry out his keyboard.
Soon, the boys were all standing and waiting on the
sidewalk in front of the store.

"Where's Reb Velvel already?" Shaya asked looking
up and down the street. "I don't see any sign of him or
his car."

"Me neither," said Yossi.

"Don't worry, guys," Gavriel said. "If Reb Velvel said
he's coming, he will come very soon."

"I never imagined that he knew how to drive at all,"
Moshe Chaim said.

"Yeah," agreed Binyamin. "What kind of car do you
think he drives anyway?"

"He called it a wonderful car," said Yossi, "so it must
be really nice."

"Do you think it's one of those new firewheels?"
Moshe Chaim asked. "My neighbor has one of those.
It's red and looks like it can go a hundred miles an
hour."

"I doubt it," said Shaya. "An old man like Reb Velvel
probably has a nice, comfortable, slow-moving car,
something like your father's new Buick. I would guess
that it would be a nice quiet color, like black or gray."

"I bet it's blue," said Binyamin.

"Wait a minute," cried Gavriel. "What's that noise?"

"What a racket!" yelled Shaya as he covered his ears. "It sounds like a broken garbage truck . . . or something even worse."

"It is worse!" cried Moshe Chaim, pointing his finger. "Look!"

Moving slowly up the street, spewing blue smoke from its tailpipe, came the ugliest car the boys had ever seen.

The entire body of the car was covered with rust, and it made a very loud noise as it rattled down the street. The boys were amazed that such a car could move at all.

Sitting behind the wheel with a big happy smile on his face was none other than Reb Velvel.

"Hop in, boys!" he yelled over the noise of the engine.

"Can we put our equipment in the trunk?" asked Gavriel.

"I'm sorry," said Reb Velvel, "but the trunk doesn't open. You'll have to keep your instruments in the car."

"What about my drums?" shouted Moshe Chaim. "How in the world am I going to keep them on the seat? There won't be any room for us."

"Don't worry," said Reb Velvel. "There's plenty of room. Just climb into the back seat, and I'll hand you your instruments."

"Okay," replied Moshe Chaim. "If you say so."

Moshe Chaim, Binyamin and Yossi climbed into the back seat.

"I don't think there's room for Shaya and me back there," said Gavriel.

"You're right," said Reb Velvel. "You two can sit in the front with me, but first we have to hand the other boys their instruments."

The sitting space of Moshe Chaim, Binyamin and Yossi in the car seemed to be getting smaller and smaller as the back seat filled up with an accordion and pieces of a drum set.

"Ugh!" cried Moshe Chaim from under a drum. "I can't move back here."

"That's nothing," cried Yossi from under an even bigger drum. "I can't breathe!"

"I think your elbow is in my ear," yelled Binyamin from under Yossi's accordion.

"All right," said Reb Velvel looking at his watch. "It's getting late, so we'd better get moving."

Gavriel and Shaya grabbed the keyboard and clambered into the front seat with it.

"Is everybody okay?" Reb Velvel asked as he pulled the car away from the curb.

"No!" cried Binyamin. "But don't worry. Just keep driving. We're in a hurry."

Suddenly, a muffled scream was heard from the back seat.

"What's the matter, Moshe Chaim?" Gavriel asked.

"We forgot something!" Moshe Chaim answered.

"What did we forget?" asked Shaya.

"Something very important," declared Moshe Chaim.

"What is it already?" Gavriel asked. "What did we forget?"

"We forgot our suits!" Moshe Chaim cried.

"Oh no!" shrieked all the other boys.

"Don't worry," said Reb Velvel. "I'll just have to drive you boys to your homes, so you can pick up your suits."

"Are you sure you wouldn't mind?" Shaya asked politely.

"No," answered Reb Velvel. "I wouldn't mind at all."

Boom! Bang! Boom! went the ancient car as it rattled down the street.

It was certainly not a very comfortable ride for the people inside.

The head of every person on the street turned to see what the source of all the noise was.

"This is so embarrassing!" Moshe Chaim whispered to Binyamin. "The whole neighborhood is watching us drive around in this noisy, beat-up clunker."

"I'd rather ride in this beat-up, old clunker than walk," Binyamin whispered back.

"That's true," agreed Moshe Chaim.

Slowly, the rusty, old car made its way to the Weintraub house. Gavriel and Binyamin ran upstairs to change into their suits.

Within a matter of minutes the two brothers returned to the car. Reb Velvel pulled the car away from the curb and headed for Shaya's house.

Suddenly, the boys heard a sound that made their hearts stop.

Clang!

"What was that noise?" asked Gavriel nervously.

"I think we just lost a piece of the car," Reb Velvel answered. "Could you please go check, Gavriel?"

Let's Do It Again!

Gavriel opened the car door and clambered out of his seat. He looked back at the road they had just driven over.

Lying in the middle of the street was a huge piece of metal.

"I think the fender fell off!" he shouted to Reb Velvel over the sound of the car's noisy engine.

"Well," said Reb Velvel scratching his head, "I would think that leaving one's fender lying on the road is not very polite. Please bring it into the car, Gavriel. I will have to get it fixed another day."

"Oh no!" shouted Moshe Chaim from under his drum. "There's hardly any room in this car as it is. How in the world are you going to fit that piece of metal in here?"

"Sorry, guys," Gavriel said as he heaved the fender into the car. "This piece of metal is going to have to fit in here somewhere."

"That's easy enough for you to say," groaned Binyamin from under an accordion and car fender.

One by one, the car pulled up to the houses of each member of the band. Each boy painfully climbed out and ran inside to change into his suit and tie. As they pulled away from Yossi Belsky's house, they heard another frightening sound.

Pow! went the car from under the hood.

"What was that?" cried Shaya.

"Oh, it was probably nothing," said Reb Velvel. "Nothing at all."

"Then what's all that white smoke coming out from under the hood?" asked Moshe Chaim.

The Cheery Bim Band

"That happens sometimes," answered Reb Velvel calmly. "It's nothing to worry about. Nothing at all."

"Oh great!" Moshe Chaim whispered to Binyamin. "Now we have blue smoke coming from the back of the car and white smoke from the front. I hope nothing else happens."

One block later, they heard another clanging noise.

"I think," said Reb Velvel, "that the car just lost its radiator. Would you mind going outside to check, Gavriel?"

"*Oy!*" groaned Moshe Chaim. "This car is falling apart faster than my mother's crumb cake! I hope we get to the *Hachnassas Sefer Torah* in one piece."

The car rattled to a stop at a red light.

"No!" moaned Yossi. "I think I'm going to faint."

"Why? What's wrong?" asked Binyamin with concern as Shaya and Gavriel turned around in their seat to try to see if Yossi was all right.

"Just look out the window," responded Yossi.

The boys all turned to see what Yossi was pointing at.

On the curb next to them was a group of boys from the seventh grade walking together to the *Hachnassas Sefer Torah.*

Shuey Waxman and Avi Gross waved merrily as they stood beside Asher Kaplan and Daniel Brickman, who were doubled over in laughter.

Just then, the light turned green, much to the relief of the Cheery Bim Band.

Suddenly, Reb Velvel stopped the car. He leaned out of his window and waved.

"What now?" groaned the boys.

"Oh no," moaned the boys in unison when they saw with whom Reb Velvel was talking.

On the sidewalk across the street stood Rabbi Feldman the school principal. He, too, was walking towards the *Hachnassas Sefer Torah*.

The five boys tried to sink lower in their seats so as not to be seen, but it was to no avail.

"Ah, Rabbi Feldman," Reb Velvel declared with pride. "You see who I have the *zchus* to be driving with today, don't you? It's the Cheery Bim Band from your own seventh grade. Such diamonds one can find in your school!"

Rabbi Feldman smiled and waved. The boys waved back weakly as Reb Velvel pulled away.

Finally, after what seemed to the boys to be a very long time, the car pulled up in front of Beis Knesses Hagadol.

Gavriel looked at his watch in amazement. Surprisingly enough, they were early.

"Thank you very much, Reb Velvel," the boys said as they climbed painfully out of the car.

"It was my pleasure," he answered with a smile. "Just make sure that you play your music *besimchah* today. Make sure you keep everyone very happy as they dance around that *Sefer Torah*. Okay?"

"Okay," they answered. "We'll try."

The boys looked up at the old *shul* standing before them. Sitting on a small, grassy hill, the huge building appeared to be bigger than their *yeshivah*. It had been constructed by the first members of Riverport's Jewish community over one hundred years earlier. The *shul* was made of huge black stones and had a large iron Jewish star perched proudly on its roof.

For many years, this had been the only *shul* in town. On *Shabbos*, a crowd of over four hundred families could be found *davening* under its roof. In later years, however, the younger families of Riverport began moving towards the other end of town, and they built their own, newer *shuls*. More and more families continued to move, and it did not take long before this once crowded *shul* was left with only a handful of aged worshippers.

All year long they would *daven* in the smaller *shul* in the bottom of the building. The huge main *shul* upstairs was only used on *Yamim Tovim* and special occasions. Only then could a crowd of any size be found gathering in this beautiful, old place of worship.

The new *Sefer Torah* had been purchased by the proud remaining members of the *shul*. There had been a need for a new *Sefer Torah* for many years now, and on this day, when it had finally arrived, there was cause for great celebration. The whole town was expected to come share in the *simchah*.

"We'd better go inside," said Gavriel glancing at his watch. "We still have to set up our equipment."

"Where are we going to be playing?" asked Shaya. "In the main *shul* or in the small *shul* downstairs?"

"I don't know," Gavriel answered. "But I see Mr. Kramer standing by the door. Let's go ask him."

The boys picked up some of their equipment and headed for the building's front door.

Let's Do It Again!

"Hi, Zeidie," Moshe Chaim called to his grandfather."

"Hello, Moshe Chaim! Hello, boys! I'm so glad you could come play for us today."

"Guess what, Zeidie!" Moshe Chaim said. "I got a ninety-eight on my *Chumash* test today."

"That's wonderful!" said Mr. Kramer happily. "I'm very proud of you, Moshe Chaim."

"Excuse me, Mr. Kramer," Gavriel interrupted. "Could you please tell us in which part of the *shul* we will be playing?"

"To be honest," Mr. Kramer chuckled, "I must tell you that you will not be setting up your equipment in any part of the *shul* at all."

The boys were all shocked. They couldn't believe what they had just heard.

"But, Zeidie!" Moshe Chaim cried. "I thought you said they wanted our band to play today!"

"I did say that," Mr. Kramer answered.

"So why did you just say that we're not going to be playing in the *shul*?"

"Your band won't be playing in the *shul*," Mr. Kramer chuckled. "You will be playing somewhere else instead."

"Where?" asked Gavriel.

"Right this very minute, the members of our *shul's* Ladies League are setting up refreshments in Mr. Fineman's backyard."

"What?" cried Moshe Chaim. "Are you saying that we are going to be playing over at Mr. Fineman's house?"

175

"Why yes," answered Mr. Kramer. "Is there a problem?"

"Er . . . no," stammered Moshe Chaim, trying very hard not to remember his last visit with Mr. Fineman. "There's no problem. No problem at all."

Suddenly, Mr. Kramer glanced down at his watch. "Oh my goodness!" he cried. "If we don't hurry up we'll be late. We'd better head for Mr. Fineman's house really quick."

"Wait a minute!" cried Gavriel. "Mr. Fineman lives three blocks away. We can't carry our equipment so far."

"Don't worry, Gavriel," said Mr. Kramer breaking into a run. "Just leave your equipment here, and I'll have someone bring it over later."

"Okay," said the boys as they sprinted after Moshe Chaim's grandfather.

"Wow!" Shaya panted. "I didn't know old men could run so fast."

"Neither did I," Moshe Chaim huffed back.

It wasn't long before the group found itself in Mr. Fineman's backyard.

"This," explained Mr. Kramer, "is where the *sofer* will finish writing the new *Sefer Torah*. When it is complete, we will dance around the new *Sefer Torah* and escort it into the *shul*."

"How come the *sofer* didn't finish writing it yet?" Yossi asked. "Didn't he have enough time until now?"

"Don't worry," Mr. Kramer chuckled. "The *sofer* had plenty of time to finish writing the *Sefer Torah*. But, you see, boys, we asked the *sofer* to leave the last few *pesukim* in the *Sefer Torah* unwritten."

"What?" cried Moshe Chaim. "You mean you want the *shul* to have a new *Sefer Torah* with some of the words missing?"

"I thought a *Sefer Torah* wasn't kosher if it was missing a word," remarked Gavriel.

"You're right, Gavriel," Mr. Kramer replied. "It is not kosher, if even the smallest letter is missing."

"So why did you ask the *sofer* to leave out the last *pesukim*?"

"We did it," answered Mr. Kramer, "so that the members of our *shul* and of our community would have the honor of writing the letters into the *Sefer Torah* themselves."

"Oh!" exclaimed Shaya. "I get it. Everyone is going to come out to this tent and watch as the last letters are written into the *Sefer Torah*."

"That is correct," answered Mr. Kramer with a smile.

"I still don't get it," said Moshe Chaim. "Aren't we supposed to be bringing this new *Sefer Torah* into the *shul*?"

"Yes," answered Mr. Kramer. "When it is complete, we will all sing and dance as we walk with it to the *shul*."

"Wait a minute!" cried Gavriel. "We can't walk with all of our equipment. How in the world are we going to play?"

"Aha!" said Mr. Kramer. "I guess it's time for me to tell you about my surprise."

"What surprise, Zeidie?" asked Moshe Chaim.

"I'll tell you what, boys," he replied. "Why don't you

all walk over to that fence at the other end of the yard? When you get there, I'll show you my surprise. Okay?"

The boys all shrugged their shoulders.

"Okay," they answered, and they began to walk to the other end of the yard.

"What do you think the surprise is?" Gavriel asked Moshe Chaim.

"I don't know," answered Moshe Chaim. "But I hope it's something to eat. I'm getting pretty hungry."

When the boys reached the fence, they stood and waited patiently for Mr. Kramer to come.

Suddenly, they heard a tremendous rumbling sound.

"What was that?" asked Shaya.

"It sounded like a train to me," answered Moshe Chaim.

He stuck his head out over the wooden fence railing.

"Whatever it is," he said, "it's coming down the road on the other side of this fence."

Suddenly, the boys heard the honk of a very loud horn.

They were surprised to see a huge red truck come barreling down the road.

Moshe Chaim felt like fainting when he saw the head that popped out of the driver's window. It was none other than his own grandfather, Mr. Kramer.

"Zeidie!" he yelled, as the truck came to a stop. "What are you doing in there? I didn't know that you knew how to drive a truck."

"This is my surprise," answered Mr. Kramer. "Look what's on the back."

Let's Do It Again!

The boys looked over at the rear of the truck.

"Hey," said Binyamin, "there's our equipment."

"That's right," said Mr. Kramer.

"Should we start loading it off the truck now?" Gavriel asked.

"No, no," Mr. Kramer chuckled. "You don't have to take your equipment off this truck."

"We don't?" asked Shaya.

"No," answered Mr. Kramer.

"But don't we have to set it up?"

"It is set up already," answered Mr. Kramer with a grin. "This afternoon, the Cheery Bim Band is going to be playing its music on the back of this truck."

"Really?" Gavriel cried.

"Yes, indeed," answered Mr. Kramer. "This way you boys will be able to lead the crowd as we walk the *Sefer Torah* over to the *shul*."

"Oh wow!" the boys cried. "That's great."

"Whoops!" said Mr. Kramer, looking at his watch. "It's getting late, and I've got to help the ladies set up the refreshments."

"We can help, too," Gavriel volunteered.

"That's very nice of you," said Mr. Kramer. "Come on then. Let's get to work. People are going to start coming any minute now."

CHAPTER

TEN

Mazel Tov

Along the sides of the Fineman family's backyard stood long tables, covered with plate upon plate of cake and other baked goods. The members of the Beis Knesses Hagadol Ladies League frantically scurried to and fro with the heaping trays, trying very hard to replace every tray as it was emptied from the table.

For these older women, this was a day of pride. Their *shul* was getting a new *Sefer Torah*, and they were determined that everyone would have a share in their joy. No one was to leave their *simchah* with an empty stomach.

"*Ess*, eat a little more cake," Mrs. Goldblatt would say.

"*Oy*, you look so skinny. Just take von more piece, it vouldn't hurt."

"This is vonderful cake that the ladies baked," Mrs.

Let's Do It Again!

Cooperstein declared proudly. "Mine five grandchildren *b'li ayin hora* love mine cake especially. Try it, you vill love it, too."

The members of the Cheery Bim Band tiptoed over to the center of the yard, where a large crowd had gathered to watch the *sofer* put the finishing touches on the *Sefer Torah.*

"Wow!" gasped Moshe Chaim. "Just about the whole neighborhood is here."

The boys all greeted their parents and squeezed into the crowd to get a better look at what was going on.

They saw a young man with a long black beard sitting over the *Sefer Torah.* His forehead was creased with concentration, as he outlined each letter.

In his hand was a long feather pen. He would carefully outline a letter on the parchment before him and then hand the quill to a member of the community to fill in the letter.

It is a great *mitzvah* to write a *Sefer Torah,* and everyone wanted to have a share. A long line of men stood waiting for their chance to fill in a letter.

Rav Michelstein, a world famous *talmid chacham* and the *rosh yeshivah* of Riverport's Beis Medrash L'Torah, had arrived. He was to be given the honor of writing in the final letter of the *Sefer Torah* and carrying it to the *shul.*

"Wow!" Gavriel whispered to Shaya. "I didn't know that Rav Michelstein was going to be here today."

Suddenly, Mr. Fineman came running over to the boys.

"You'd better get ready to play," he whispered. "The *Sefer Torah* is almost finished."

Moshe Chaim felt a hand on his shoulder. He turned to see his father standing behind him. Yehoshua Kramer gave his son a big hug.

"Moshe Chaim," he began, "I want you to know that I'm not at all surprised that you got a good mark on your *Chumash* test today. You are a very smart boy, and I expect you to learn well. Once I saw you working really hard on your learning, I was sure you would succeed. I'm very, very proud of you."

"Thanks," Moshe Chaim said as a warm feeling of pride filled his chest. "I'll speak to you more about it later. Right now I have to get ready to play with the band. Okay?"

"Wait a minute, Moshe Chaim!" his father stopped him. "I forgot to give you something."

"What is it?" asked Moshe Chaim.

Mr. Kramer handed his son a big brown garbage bag. "In here," he said, "are all those posters and business cards that you worked on so hard."

Moshe Chaim smiled.

Gavriel and Shaya came up behind Moshe Chaim just in time to catch his last words.

"Thanks," Moshe Chaim said, winking at his father. "But I don't think we really need the posters and cards after all. I think they were all just a waste of time anyway."

"I'm glad to hear you say that, Moshe Chaim."

Shaya and Gavriel exchanged glances as Moshe Chaim went off to find Yossi and Binyomin.

Let's Do It Again!

"I don't think it was all a waste of time," declared Gavriel.

"We can certainly fix it so that it won't be," Shaya agreed.

The two boys went over to Mr. Kramer to hold a whispered conference.

A few minutes later, Moshe Chaim reappeared with Yossi and Binyamin.

"Hey, Moshe Chaim," called a voice from the roof of the truck.

Moshe Chaim looked up and saw his huge banner propped up across the top of the truck cab. "CHEERY BIM BAND, Music for Every Occasion," it read in huge black and red letters.

Moshe Chaim beamed with pride.

"It does look pretty good, doesn't it?" he declared.

"Sure does!" all the boys agreed.

"Now, I wouldn't call that a waste of time exactly," Gavriel said from behind the sign where he was busy securing it.

"No, I guess not," Moshe Chaim said thoughtfully. "I guess you just have to know when it's the right time for things."

The boys all smiled and nodded. Gavriel and Shaya slid down into the back of the truck as the boys began to eagerly prepare their instruments, waiting for Gavriel's signal.

"Are you ready, guys?" Gavriel asked his friends.

They all nodded their heads.

This was it, the moment they had all been waiting for.

The Cheery Bim Band

The crowd grew quiet as Rabbi Michelstein wrote in the final letter of the *Sefer Torah*. When he was finished, cries of *"Mazel Tov!"* filled the air.

With a radiant smile on his face, Mr. Fineman turned toward the band and waved his hand wildly.

Gavriel gazed happily into the eyes of all his friends.

"Okay, guys," he whispered. "We'll start on the count of three. One . . . and a two . . . and a *three!*"

Moshe Chaim started a very fast paced drumroll, and the boys began their music.

"Simen tov umazel tov yehay lanu, simen tov umazel tov yehay lanu ulechal Yisrael . . ."

Rabbi Michelstein lovingly rolled up the *Sefer Torah*, tied the belt around it and placed it carefully in its embroidered velvet covering.

"Simen tov umazel tov yehay lanu ulechal Yisrael, amen."

A clapping crowd of men gathered around the *rosh yeshivah* as he picked up the *Sefer Torah* and laid it gently on his shoulder. He smiled at the people and began to dance around and around.

"Simen tov umazel tov . . ."

Faster and faster, the men clapped, as Rav Michelstein twirled around and around with the *Sefer Torah* in his hands.

"Simen tov umazel tov yehay lanu ulechal Yisrael . . ."

Mr. Fineman grabbed Mr. Kramer's hands, and the two old men danced around the *rosh yeshivah*. The other men in the crowd then formed a much larger circle around them.

Let's Do It Again!

The women stood off to the side, watching proudly as every man and boy locked hands and danced.

Gavriel turned toward Shaya.

"Take the solo," he whispered.

"Uh uh," answered Shaya, nervously shaking his head from side to side. "Why don't we let Moshe Chaim sing? After all, he's the guy who did so great on his *Chumash* test today."

Gavriel smiled and motioned toward Moshe Chaim. Moshe Chaim nodded, grabbed a microphone and began to sing.

"*Simen tov umazel tov yehay lanu simen tov umazel tov yehay lanu ulechal Yisrael . . .*"

When he had finished singing, Moshe Chaim was surprised to hear someone standing right in front of him begin to clap.

He looked down from the truck to see none other than Rabbi Goldsmith himself standing and clapping with a proud smile across his lips.

Soon, it was time for a new song, and without missing a beat, the Cheery Bim Band began one.

"*Torah Torah Torah, tziva lanu Moshe, morashah kehilas Yaakov . . .*"

Everyone looked on in amazement as Mr. Fineman took the *Sefer Torah* from the *rosh yeshivah* and began to jump up and down with it. His feet moved as if they belonged to a twelve-year-old boy.

"*Torah Torah Torah, tziva lanu Moshe, morashah kehilas Yaakov . . .*"

Suddenly, Binyamin's eyes lit up.

"Wow!" he whispered. "Look at that!"

The boys all looked down from the truck to see old Mr. Kramer crouching down to the ground and kicking his feet high up into the air.

"I don't believe it," cried Moshe Chaim. "My grandfather is dancing the *kazatzka*."

"*Oyy . . . Torah Torah Torah . . .*"

Gavriel found himself feeling dizzy as he watched the huge circle of men dancing round and round. In a way, he wished he could join the happy crowd of men in their joyous dance around the *Sefer Torah*. He knew, however, that his fingers dancing back and forth across the keyboard produced a far greater *simchah*. The dance of his fingers brought a joy to each and every person in the crowd as they listened.

"*. . . Tziva lanu Moshe . . .*"

Shaya's face was red, and his glasses were fogged with sweat, but he didn't care. He was making hundreds of people happy in honor of the *Sefer Torah*. What more could he possibly want?

"*Morashah kehilas Yaakov . . .*"

Gavriel jabbed Binyamin with his elbow. "Look who's coming into the yard," he whispered.

Binyamin lifted his flute and was surprised to see his oldest brother Avraham, who learned and slept in a *yeshivah* high school in Brooklyn.

Avraham had brought a group of friends with him from his *yeshivah*, and now this bunch of bright, young men eagerly joined the dancing.

"Let's start playing some dance music!" Yossi suggested.

"That's a great idea," agreed Gavriel. "Let's play that

Let's Do It Again!

Mordechai Ben David song *Daaga Menayin.* One . . . and a two . . . and a *three!"*

"Heh-avar ayin, vihe-asid adayin, vihe-hoveh kiheref ayin daaga menayin . . ."

A cry of joy went up from the young boys in the crowd. This was a song to which they all loved to dance.

The older men stepped back, happy to take a short rest as a sea of black-hatted, young heads rushed to take their place in the dance circle.

Moshe Chaim was unbelievably happy. When he had awakened that morning, he had not even been a member of the band, and now he was playing in front of his *rebbi,* the *rosh yeshivah* and practically the whole town of Riverport. *Baruch Hashem,* everything had worked out just great.

"Vihe-hoveh kiheref ayin, daaga menayin . . ."

"Hey, guys!" Gavriel called. "Let's play our new song!"

"Oh yeah!"

"Let's do it!"

"One . . . and a two . . . and a *three!"*

The music started. It sounded very much like the popular song *Veyazor Veyagain.* The words, however, were completely different.

> Thunder and lightning all around a mountain
>   called Har Sinai.
> The call of the shofar shook the ground
>   and echoed through the sky.
> Naaseh venishma, we all said,
>   Hashem's laws we will obey.

The Cheery Bim Band

And that's why we all lead our lives
the holy Torah's way.

(chorus)
> *EITZ CHAIM HEE LAMACHAZIKIM BAH*
> *VESOMCHEHA MEUSHAR.*
> THE TORAH IS OUR TREE
> A TREE OF LIFE FROM THE ONE ABOVE
> A SPECIAL GIFT TO YOU AND ME
> THAT HASHEM GAVE TO US WITH LOVE.
>
> EVERYBODY'S GOTTA LEARN . . .
> GOTTA LEARN SOME TORAH
> CHIRRY BIM CHIRRY BUM,
> CHIRRY BIM BUM BIM BUM BUM.

The dancing stopped as everyone paused to listen to the beautiful new words sung to the popular tune. The crowd clapped wildly in time to the music. The *rosh yeshivah* grabbed the *Sefer Torah* and made his way to the center of the circle once again.

"Let's play *Veyazor* again," Gavriel whispered to his friends, "and this time let's use the regular words."

"*Veyazor veyagain veyoshia lechol hachosim hachosim bo . . .*"

The members of the band were startled to hear the sound of the truck's engine starting up.

"Hang on, boys!" Mr. Kramer shouted from the driver's seat. "We're going to swing around the block and meet the crowd in front of the house."

The boys held tightly to both the side of the truck and their instruments as they turned onto the road.

Let's Do It Again!

By the time the truck rounded the corner and pulled up in front of the house, the crowd was already piling onto the street.

"*Veyazor veyagain veyoshia lechol hachosim hachosim bo . . .*"

The people quickly fell in line behind Rav Michelstein, who stood dancing with the *Sefer Torah* under a *chupah* held aloft by four dancing men.

A patrol car from the Riverport police force stood waiting on every street corner, halting traffic so the huge crowd could pass.

The boys felt so proud, standing high atop the truck bed leading the crowd as they played.

Soon, the crowd reached its destination, Beis Knesses Hagadol.

Mr. Fineman came running over to the truck.

"You'd better get ready, boys," he panted. "We're going to dance the *Sefer Torah* up the stairs and into the *shul.*"

"Uh oh," exclaimed Moshe Chaim. "How in the world am I supposed to carry my drums around the *shul?*"

"I have the same problem with my keyboard," said Gavriel. "I guess we'll just have to stay with our instruments here in the truck."

"Yossi, Binyamin and I can play as we walk," said Shaya. "Our instruments aren't heavy at all."

"Speak for yourself," moaned Yossi, as he strained to stand up with his accordion.

"Can you make it, Yossi?" Gavriel asked.

"Yeah," he sighed. "I guess I can try."

The Cheery Bim Band

"Okay," said Gavriel. "Let's start a new song here on the truck before they take the *Sefer Torah* inside."

"One . . . and a two . . . and a *three! Moshe emes, Moshe emes, vesoraso emes . . .*"

Rav Michelstein's eyes were closed, and a broad smile was spread across his lips as he danced with the *Sefer Torah* up the path leading to the *shul*.

"*Moshe emes, Moshe emes, vesoraso emes . . .*"

The ancient black stones of Beis Knesses Hagadol seemed to smile with pride as hundreds of eager smiling faces danced up its stone walk.

"*Moshe emes, Moshe emes, visoraso emes . . .*"

Most of these people had lived in Riverport all of their lives. For decades, their parents and grandparents had come to this beautiful, old building to pour their hearts out to their Creator.

How many babies had had their *bris milah* under the shelter of these large black stones? How many *barmitzvahs* had taken place behind these tall, wooden doors?

Beis Knesses Hagadol had played a very important role in the history of almost every family in town.

And now, up these hallowed stone stairs danced the mob of people singing a new chorus with each step.

When Rav Michelstein reached the entrance to the building he stopped and lifted the *Sefer Torah* high into the air and danced back and forth across the building's long front stoop.

The crowd then squeezed into the building's front doors and formed a circle in the *shul's* hallway.

Shaya, Yossi and Binyamin stood on the outside of

the circle with the sounds of happy music flowing nonstop from their instruments.

Shaya was sweating so much that he thought he needed windshield wipers for his glasses. He was dripping wet from head to toe, but his mouth refused to stop blowing into his beloved clarinet.

Suddenly, Shaya felt a hand grab his arm. He didn't know what was happening. He felt himself being pulled closer and closer to the center of the circle, but he would not stop playing.

Finally, Shaya lifted his eyes to see a sight that almost made him faint. Standing no less than a foot away, directly in front of him, was none other than Rav Michelstein.

Shaya's tired body found a new burst of energy. His legs started to dance up a storm as his lips continued to blow into the clarinet. He simply couldn't believe it. Here he was, dancing with the world famous *rosh yeshivah*. This was going to be one dance he would never forget.

"*Moshe emes . . . visoraso emes . . .*"

Binyamin and Yossi continued their playing on the outside of the circle until they, too, felt themselves being pulled into the center.

The two friends looked up at each other and smiled. There was only one thing for them to do.

Binyamin stuck out his left hand and locked it around Yossi's. The two friends then spun together around Rav Michelstein and Shaya in time to the music they were playing.

"*Moshe emes . . . visoraso emes . . .*"

The Cheery Bim Band

Gavriel and Moshe Chaim watched happily from the outside of the circle as their friends danced around the *rosh yeshivah*.

Suddenly, they each felt a hand tugging at their arms. Gavriel looked up to see Reb Velvel pulling him and Moshe Chaim towards the center of the dancing circle.

Once inside, he and the members of the band formed a small dancing circle of their own around Rav Michelstein and the *Sefer Torah*.

This is amazing, thought Moshe Chaim to himself as he reached up to kiss the *Sefer Torah*. Just a few days ago, I thought I would never be a part of the band again, and now I'm dancing with a world famous *talmid chacham* like Rav Michelstein. I just can't believe it!

Finally, it was time to bring the *Sefer Torah* into the *shul* itself. The double doors were swung open, and the crowd squeezed itself between them.

When he stepped inside, Gavriel couldn't help but stop and stare in awe and wonder at the beautiful sight before him.

His eyes followed the high curved walls all the way up. This room was taller than his house. It almost seemed to be as tall as one of the buildings in the city.

Hanging from the top of the ceiling were three big, beautiful crystal chandeliers, each of which appeared to be bigger than the truck the boys had just been on.

Standing before the dancing crowd of people was a sea of long, wooden benches. There were enough seats in this *shul* for the whole town.

The dancing crowd of people squeezed through the

192

narrow aisle between the benches and made its way toward the front of the room.

As they approached the front of the *shul*, Gavriel gazed up at the *aron hakodesh*, in which the *Sefer Torah* was to be placed.

It was magnificent.

At its top, just below the *shul*'s ceiling, stood two golden lions holding up a pair of purple and gold *luchos*. Below this was a beautiful cluster of carved wooden flowers atop four tall, wooden pillars. At the base of the *aron*, there were five wooden steps leading up to the beautiful gold curtain that covered its doors.

"Hey, Shaya," Gavriel whispered to his friend. "Rav Michelstein is about to go up the steps to the *aron*. Why don't you guys play *Siu Shearim*, the song we sing on *Simchas Torah* when the *Sifrei Torah* are put away?"

Shaya nodded his head eagerly in agreement.

He motioned to Binyamin and Yossi, and the new song began.

"*Siu shearim rasheychem vehinasu pischei olam . . .*"

The men and boys all locked arms and formed a long dancing line before the approaching *Sefer Torah*.

"*Veyavo Melech hakavod . . . Hakavod Selah . . .*"

Back and forth they danced between the *Sefer Torah* and the *aron* with each and every face in the room shining brightly with happiness.

As Rav Michelstein approached the stairs leading up to the *aron*, the singing reached a feverish pitch. The sound of clapping hands echoed loudly off of the *shul's* high ceiling.

The Cheery Bim Band

After each step up, Rav Michelstein turned toward the singing crowd and waved his hand in time to the music.

When he finally reached the top step, he pulled aside the *aron's* golden curtain and slid open its polished, wooden doors. Then, the *rosh yeshivah* raised the *Sefer Torah* high into the air and broke out into one last joyous dance.

Rav Michelstein lovingly kissed the *Sefer Torah* and gently placed it among the others in the *aron*. There it would wait until the arrival of the approaching *Yom Tov* of *Shavuos*, when it would be taken out and read before the members of the *shul* for the very first time.

When the music stopped, everyone rushed to find a seat, for on this important occasion the people of Riverport were in for a special treat. Rav Michelstein, the world famous *rosh yeshivah*, was going to address them with some words of Torah.

Moshe Chaim Kramer smiled at his father as Rav Michelstein spoke about the importance of setting aside time for Torah learning. He had learned that lesson very well over the past week and was determined never to forget it.

The *rosh yeshivah* then spoke about the love and respect that all Jews should have for one another and how hard they should try to avoid fighting with one another.

Gavriel smiled to himself as he gazed up at the huge balcony which held the *shul's* ladies' section. Somewhere up there sat his little sister Dassie. She was a good girl, and he had treated her very badly over the past week. He had accused her of taking his papers, and he had been wrong. From now on, Gavriel was determined to treat her a lot nicer.

Not a sound was heard in the packed *shul* as the *rosh yeshivah* spoke. Every person in the room sat listening intently, eagerly drinking in the words of wisdom from the famous *talmid chacham*.

When he finished speaking, the music started up once again, and a new dancing circle of men was formed.

This was certainly a day that would live in the memory of the people of Riverport for many years to come.

CHAPTER ELEVEN

Let's Learn

It was eleven o'clock *Shavuos* night. The sounds of footsteps echoed loudly through the quiet streets of Riverport as Mr. Weintraub and his sons made their way to *shul*.

While everyone else was lying down for a good night's sleep, Jewish men and boys all over the world were heading for their *shul* or *beis medrash* to begin a long night of Torah learning.

The streets were very dark and deserted, so Gavriel and Binyamin stood close to their father, but they couldn't help but chatter excitedly as they walked.

"I love *Shavuos*," said Gavriel. "It's so exciting to stay up the whole night."

"Yeah," said Binyamin rubbing his stomach, "and when we get home, we get to have cheesecake with our *Kiddush*."

Let's Do It Again!

"Those things are very nice to do," said Mr. Weintraub, "but just don't forget the most important part of *Shavuos*, the Torah learning."

"Oh," cried Gavriel, "we would never forget that. The whole point of *Shavuos* is to remember how we got the Torah at Har Sinai."

"I'm very glad to hear you say that, Gavriel, and I've also been meaning to compliment you on the wonderful way you've been acting toward your sister. You've been getting along so nicely with her these past few days."

"Yeah," agreed Binyamin. "It's so nice not to have a house full of fights anymore."

When they arrived at *shul*, Gavriel quickly grabbed a *Gemara* and took a seat next to Shaya.

"Good *yom tov*, Gavriel," Shaya happily greeted his friend.

"Good *yom tov*, Shaya. How are you doing?"

"I'm doing great. Everyone keeps coming over to me and telling me how great the band was at the *Hachnassas Sefer Torah*."

"Yeah," said Gavriel. "The same thing keeps happening to me. I guess we did a pretty good job."

"A good job?" came a voice from behind them. "What do you mean we did a good job? We did a great job."

Gavriel and Shaya turned around to see Moshe Chaim standing behind them with a *Gemara* in his hand.

"Good *yom tov*, Moshe Chaim," they both cried together. "Pull up a chair and join us."

The Cheery Bim Band

"So what do you think, guys?" Moshe Chaim began as he sat down beside them. "When is the Cheery Bim Band going to play next? Do you think we'll get another chance when summer starts?"

"I sure hope so," said Gavriel. "If we're not going away to camp until August, we'd better have something to do with ourselves."

"Well, if I know you, Gavriel," said Moshe Chaim with a laugh, "you'll think of something."

"Hey, guys," cried Shaya. "We're supposed to be learning now, not talking about the band."

"You're right," agreed Moshe Chaim. "I made up my mind this week that I wasn't going to do that again."

"So," said Gavriel, "let's learn!"

The three friends smiled at one another, opened their *Gemaras* and happily began to do what Jews have been doing since they got the Torah on Har Sinai, so many years ago. They sat and learned.

Glossary

ammos: cubit measures

aron: ark

bar-mitzvah: adulthood

Baruch Hashem: Blessed is the Name; thank Heaven

becher: goblet [Yiddish]

beis medrash: study hall

Beis Hamikdash: Holy Temple in Jerusalem

beis din: rabbinical court

bentch: to bless

b'li ayin hara: without the evil eye

brachah: blessing

challah (challos): *Shabbos* loaves

chas veshalom: Heaven forbid

Chol Hamoed: intermediate days of the Festivals

Chumashim: Books of the Pentateuch

chupah: bridal canopy

daven: pray

Gemara: part of the Talmud

Gut vach: post-*Shabbos* greeting [Yiddish]

hamotzi: blessing over bread

Har Sinai: Mount Sinai

hasmadah: diligence

Havdalah: concluding ritual of *Shabbos*

kavanah: concentration

Kiddush: sanctification of *Shabbos* or festivals

Lag Ba'omer: thirty-third day of the *Omer*

Lecha Dodi: poem welcoming the *Shabbos*

lechem mishneh: two *Shabbos* loaves

malachim: angels

matzah: unleavened bread

minyan: quorum of ten
Mishnah: part of the Talmud
mitzvah: Torah commandment
pasuk (pesukim) : verse(s)
perek: chapter
rosh yeshivah: dean
seder: Passover feast
sefer (sefarim): book(s)
Sefer Torah: Torah scroll
seudah: feast
shalosh seudos: third *Shabbos* meal
Shavuos: Pentecost, late spring festival
shofar: ram's horn
shul: synagogue [Yiddish]
simchah: rejoicing

Simchas Torah: Festival of the Torah
siyum: conclusion
sofer: scribe
sukkah: *Sukkos* booth
talmid chacham: Torah scholar
Tehillim: Book of Psalms
tzaddik (im): righteous person (people)
yarmulka: skullcap
yasher koach: thank you
yeshivah: Torah school
yetzer hara: evil inclination
yom tov: festival
zechus: merit
zemiros: songs